FIRSTBORN SONS

PROFILE

FIRSTBORN SON:	Kyle Ramsey
AGE:	31
STATS:	6'0"; thick, wavy hair, smoldering gray eyes, broad shoulders
OCCUPATION:	Pilot
AREA OF EXPERTISE:	Top gun navy flier in the air; seductive, fly-by-night lover on the ground
PERSONALITY:	Strong, courageous, certain of his destiny…until a certain strong-willed lady shakes him to the core
FAVORITE SPORT:	Ocean swimming—pitting his strength and skill against the raging waves
MOST CHARMING CHARACTERISTIC:	Smoky bedroom eyes that whisper secret pleasures
BRAVEST ACT OF COURAGE:	Taking down a knife-wielding thug threatening an innocent young woman on a street in Nicaragua
PREFERRED ROMANTIC SETTING:	A candlelit bedroom with a soft bed and the warm, willing woman of his dreams wrapped in his arms
GREATEST PASSION:	Joanna Morgan, the woman with whom he shared one memorable night of lovemaking. The woman he can't forget….

Dear Reader,

As always, Intimate Moments offers you six terrific books to fill your reading time, starting with Terese Ramin's *Her Guardian Agent*. For FBI agent Hazel Youvella, the case that took her back to revisit her Native American roots was a very personal one. For not only did she find the hero of her heart in Native American tracker Guy Levoie, she discovered the truth about the missing child she was seeking. This wasn't just any child—this was *her* child.

If you enjoyed last month's introduction to our FIRSTBORN SONS in-line continuity, you won't want to miss the second installment. Carla Cassidy's *Born of Passion* will grip you from the first page and leave you longing for the rest of these wonderful linked books. Valerie Parv takes a side trip from Silhouette Romance to debut in Intimate Moments with a stunner of a reunion romance called *Interrupted Lullaby*. Karen Templeton begins a new miniseries called HOW TO MARRY A MONARCH with *Plain-Jane Princess,* and Linda Winstead Jones returns with *Hot on His Trail,* a book you should be hot on the trail of yourself. Finally, welcome Sharon Mignerey back and take a look at her newest, *Too Close for Comfort.*

And don't forget to look in the back of this book to see how Silhouette can make you a star.

Enjoy them all, and come back next month for more of the best and most exciting romance reading around.

Yours,

Leslie J. Wainger
Executive Senior Editor

Please address questions and book requests to:
Silhouette Reader Service
U.S.: 3010 Walden Ave., P.O. Box 1325, Buffalo, NY 14269
Canadian: P.O. Box 609, Fort Erie, Ont: L2A 5X3

BORN
OF
PASSION
Carla
Cassidy

INTIMATE MOMENTS™

Published by Silhouette Books

America's Publisher of Contemporary Romance

Special thanks and acknowledgment are given
to Carla Cassidy for her contribution
to the FIRSTBORN SONS series.

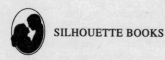 SILHOUETTE BOOKS

ISBN 0-373-27164-6

BORN OF PASSION

Copyright © 2001 by Harlequin Books S.A.

Visit Silhouette at www.eHarlequin.com

Printed in U.S.A.

Bound by the legacy of their fathers, six Firstborn Sons are about to discover the stuff true heroes—and true love—are made of....

Kyle Ramsey: When he returns to Montebello on a covert mission, this blatantly masculine Firstborn Son reunites with the exotic beauty he'd shared a night of passion with. Can this restless top-gun pilot reclaim the mother of his child?

Joanna Morgan: Out of self-preservation, this headstrong military attaché has been keeping a precious secret from her globe-trotting lover. For she yearns for the one thing an adventure-seeking Kyle can *never* give her—a place to call home.

Major Edward Ramsey: Though he's raised his boys to be all they can be, his rebellious Firstborn Son will be the one to follow in his footsteps....

King Marcus: His kindness and compassion are legendary. But this formidable ruler's kid gloves come off when his country and his kingdom are threatened!

Prince Lucas Sebastiani and Sheik Rashid Kamal: To the dismay of their families, these royal heirs are still missing in action....

A note from prolific author Carla Cassidy:

Dear Reader,

I was thrilled when I was asked to participate in another one of Silhouette's exciting continuity series. This one, FIRSTBORN SONS, was especially fun, because it deals with a powerful covert organization, handsome, daring men of action, and women strong enough to love those men.

Born of Passion begins with a one-night stand that my hero, Kyle Ramsey, can't forget and my heroine, Joanna Morgan, desperately wants to forget. One delicious, unforgettable night that stirs in these two strong people a passion that will make them fight the odds to find a lasting, forever kind of love.

I have been writing for Silhouette for the past nine years, and in that time have written over fifty books. I've been a Romance Writers of America RITA Award finalist and have won a variety of awards from *Romantic Times Magazine*.

I hope you enjoy reading *Born of Passion* as much as I enjoyed writing it.

Carla Cassidy

Chapter 1

Intoxicating.

Kyle Ramsey drew a deep breath, discerning the tang of lemon, delicate citrus blossoms and exotic spices among the many fragrances that rode the warm air that surrounded him.

Montebello. The sounds and smells of the Mediterranean island seemed to welcome him back as he grabbed his duffel bag and hopped into a taxi.

"The U.S. Embassy," he said to the driver, then settled back in the seat.

It had been three months since he'd been here, and while on the surface Montebello showed no change, Kyle knew there had been changes...changes that threatened the fiber, the very heart, of the beautiful island.

He brushed at a tiny piece of lint on the sleeve of

his naval uniform. He'd flown on a transport plane to Montebello and could have taken military transport to the embassy. But he'd opted for a taxi instead, needing time alone to think and to prepare himself for whatever responsibility lay ahead.

His commanding officer had been vague about Kyle's exact mission when he'd given him the orders to return to Montebello. He'd simply explained that the ambassador in Montebello would fill Kyle in when he arrived.

"You've come to the prettiest island in the world," the cabbie said, his dark eyes looking at Kyle through the rearview mirror.

"Have you been here long?" Kyle asked, recognizing a slight East Coast U.S. accent in the man's voice.

"Ten years. Came out here to visit a friend for a week, but somehow I never left. This island is as bewitching as a beautiful woman. Once it gets you in its grasp, you never want to be released."

The cabbie's words instantly evoked a memory in Kyle's mind—the memory of a single night with a local Montebello woman…a single night of the most mind-numbing, searing passion he'd ever experienced in his life.

They had met in a local bar, and she'd said her name was Marie. They'd spent the evening flirting outrageously with one another, performing an intense dance of courtship that had culminated in a nearby hotel room.

Although three months had passed since that crazy night, her bewitching image was still as sharply etched in his mind as it had been the first moment he'd spotted her.

Her dark brown hair had been a spill of silk to her shoulders. Her rich nut-brown eyes, with their sinfully long lashes, had flirted and danced. She'd had a heart-shaped face and full lips that had tantalized him.

Clad in a lacy white dress that emphasized not only her slender curves and long, shapely legs, but also the dark olive of her skin, she'd caught his eye the moment he'd walked into the place.

Their lovemaking had held an edge of wildness, as if they had indulged in foreplay for years instead of mere hours. When he'd finally fallen asleep with her in his arms, he'd had the feeling that for the first time in his thirty-one years, life was about to make some kind of sense.

In the morning she'd been gone, like a desert mirage that shimmered brightly in the sun, then vanished. He'd been shocked—bewildered—and surprisingly devastated.

He'd looked for her for two days, then had been called back to the States.

Now he was back in Montebello, but he didn't expect to have time to dwell on thoughts of a dark-haired beauty who had turned his world upside down for a single night.

He sat up straighter as the U.S. Embassy came into view. The building itself was imposing with thick columns and steep steps leading to the grandiose building. An American flag on a tall pole fluttered in the breeze.

The driver pulled up in front, and Kyle paid him, then picked up his duffel bag and entered the embassy through the front doors.

A metal detector and a conveyor belt instantly confronted him. Both were a vivid reminder of the marvels of technology and the state of unrest around the world. And from what the rumor mill implied, nowhere was unrest more threatening than here in Montebello.

Tensions had risen between King Marcus Sebastiani of Montebello and Sheik Ahmed Kamal of the neighboring kingdom of Tamir. The tension had reached explosive proportions a month before when a bomb had detonated in a civilian square, destroying a restaurant and trapping people inside. The people of Montebello pointed fingers of blame to Kamal, furthering increasing tensions.

After walking through the metal detector, he had his identification checked and signed in for his appointment with Ambassador Nigel Templeton.

By the time Kyle had cleared security, an assistant had appeared to lead him to the ambassador's office. "Joel Mayfield," the young man said, and held his hand out to Kyle. He had the kind of crisp, clean attractiveness that all the people who worked at the embassy seemed to possess.

"Lieutenant Commander Kyle Ramsey," Kyle replied, and firmly shook Joel's hand. With the formalities out of the way, Joel led Kyle down a long hallway to a bank of elevators, past a number of offices buzzing with activity.

"I understand this isn't your first trip to Montebello,'' the assistant said as they stepped into the elevator and he punched the button for the fifth floor.

"That's right. I was here several months ago," Kyle replied.

"It's a beautiful place, isn't it?"

Kyle nodded, and again his head filled with the vision of the beautiful woman who had given him the most memorable night of his life. He could still recall her haunting fragrance—a scent of exotic spices and a touch of citrus, as mysterious and romantic as this island itself.

Stepping out of the elevator, he shook his head, as if to physically dispel the seductive image. He needed to be clearheaded for his meeting with the ambassador. From the moment Kyle had been commanded to return to the island, he'd sensed something odd going on.

Although he'd previously met Ambassador Templeton, he'd never been in the man's inner sanctum. The assistant led him into a large waiting room, nodded to the secretary on duty at a desk, then knocked lightly on the door just behind where she sat.

Joel opened the door and gestured for Kyle to enter. The office was large and airy, a corner room with windows. Ambassador Templeton rose from behind his large, mahogany desk, his hand outstretched in greeting.

"Lieutenant Commander Ramsey," he said as they shook hands.

"It's nice to see you again, Ambassador Templeton," Kyle replied, then was waved into one of the chairs in front of the desk.

Nigel Templeton had been born in Phoenix, Arizona, though his parents were natives of Montebello. He'd grown up in the States, then his family had moved back to the island, and Nigel had begun a career in diplomacy and politics, culminating in him being appointed ambassador three years earlier.

He was a handsome man, his ethnicity apparent in his rich dark hair, deep olive skin and brown eyes, which radiated not only intelligence and dignity, but compassion as well. At the moment, his gaze was filled with worry, and lines of tension snaked across his forehead.

"Montebello is on the verge of a security crisis," he began. "I know your commanding officer told you that your mission here would be as it was when you were here before—to protect American oil interests in the Middle East. But that's not your real mission."

Kyle leaned forward, intrigued.

"I'm sure you've heard that Prince Lucas Sebastiani is missing," Ambassador Templeton continued.

Kyle nodded. "I read that his plane went down somewhere in the Colorado Rockies a couple months ago, and the search and rescue teams have yet to find his body."

"A tragic state of affairs. As you can imagine, King Marcus is beside himself with grief. Compounding that sorrow is the fact that his daughter, Princess Julia, is pregnant, and the father of the baby is reported to be Sheik Ahmed Kamal's son, Rashid."

"But I would think this good news," Kyle replied.

"A union between Princess Julia and Sheik Rashid surely would end the tensions that have existed between Montebello and Tamir."

Ambassador Templeton leaned back in his chair. "Unfortunately, Sheik Rashid has disappeared, and since he was last seen in the company of Princess Julia, Sheik Ahmed believes King Marcus had something to do with his son's disappearance. Sheik Ahmed has let King Marcus know he's prepared to take by force the land on Montebello that would have gone to Prince Lucas."

Kyle frowned thoughtfully. If the nearby kingdom of Tamir waged battle against Montebello, the fragile peace of the entire Middle East would be shattered.

Once again Ambassador Templeton leaned forward, his dark gaze intense. "Officially, you are here as you were before, to protect American oil interests. Unofficially, you and your team of top gun pilots will be patroling the air space between Montebello and Tamir. You will be on a state of high alert, anticipating a potential air strike and invasion from Tamir. You will report to only three people—King Marcus himself, me or any of the Noble Men who might contact you."

"The Noble Men?" Kyle looked at him in bewilderment.

"They are the ones who brought you here. They are the ones funding the entire mission of protection for King Marcus and Montebello."

"I don't understand. Who are these Noble Men?" Kyle felt as if the ambassador had suddenly begun to speak a foreign language.

"I'm only telling you this because King Marcus and the Noble Men agreed you should be told." He stared out the window for a long moment, where the sky was an intense, almost surreal blue. "But first I must have your word that you will keep what I tell you in total confidence."

"Of course I give you my word," Kyle said instantly, his curiosity aroused to a fever pitch.

"Nobody knows exactly who they are, and very few people know of their existence." Templeton looked back at Kyle. "What we do know is that they are a covert organization of wealthy, powerful men." His voice was filled with admiration and respect. "They are peacekeepers and protectors who save lives and restore order, often financing and planning rescue missions in situations where government hands are tied."

Kyle's head reeled with the information he'd just been handed. A covert organization, men wielding power and influence for world peace... It sounded like something from an action-adventure movie, and yet he had no reason to doubt what the ambassador had shared with him.

"You said that these Noble Men were the ones who brought me here. Why me?"

For the first time since the ambassador had greeted Kyle, he smiled. "I can't know for sure, and I wouldn't begin to question the choices the Noble Men make, but I would imagine it's because you are one of the best pilots that the United States Navy has to offer."

His smile faded. "You must understand that, officially, the United States military is not involved in this operation. Unofficially, they will allow you to use their planes and their equipment, and will provide ground support. I'm placing one of my top military attachés in charge of the ground support unit. She will be available to you day and night, whatever it takes to make this mission a success. Her name is Joanna Morgan."

The ambassador looked down at his wristwatch. "I had hoped she would join us here, but apparently she's been held up. We'd like to get twenty-four-hour patrols started as soon as possible."

He stood and Kyle did the same. "You will be staying in your family apartment?"

Kyle hesitated only a moment, then nodded. He'd have preferred to stay on the base, but apparently that wasn't where the ambassador wanted him.

"Good, then if you'll just have a seat in the reception area, I'm sure Joanna will be here momentarily. She can drive you to your apartment and you two can begin strategizing your mission."

He walked around the desk and once again held out his hand to Kyle. "Thank you, Lieutenant Commander, for being available to serve not only the Noble Men, but the people of Montebello as well."

"I look forward to getting to work immediately," Kyle replied. The two men said their goodbyes and Kyle left the office.

"May I get you a cup of coffee while you wait?" the secretary asked with a friendly smile.

"No thanks, I'm fine." Kyle sat in one of the dark

blue, upholstered chairs, wondering how long he'd have to wait for this Joanna Morgan to show.

Now that he knew exactly what his mission here would be, he was eager to get started. His mind replayed all that Nigel Templeton had told him.

Two grieving fathers—a king and a sheik—both pointing fingers at the other. If war broke out, the consequences would be felt around the world.

The Noble Men. To say that the concept of a secret organization of wealthy, influential men intrigued him would be a vast understatement. Who were they? What had driven them to form such an organization? What made some men become altruistic and idealistic, while others became fat-cat corporate heads, worshipping the almighty dollar?

He shoved away the mental picture of his father that suddenly sprang to his mind. At the moment he had more important things to think about than Edward Ramsey.

He'd given his word that he would not speak of the Noble Men, and his mind worked to figure out just what he could tell his team of flyers and what he couldn't. They needed to know only their objective, to keep the skies free of threat, and Kyle was confident they would follow his instructions without question.

A woman walked in, swiftly crossing the room to the receptionist desk. Although Kyle saw her only from the back, he couldn't help but admire the long shapely legs beneath the short navy skirt, the curvy form of her derriere and the shiny dark hair tied back at the nape of her neck.

She spoke to the receptionist, but their voices were too low for him to hear. He wondered if this woman was the one he'd been waiting for—Joanna Morgan.

When she turned around, a shock of recognition ripped through him. "Marie," he whispered. At the same time his gaze shot to the name on her badge: Joanna M. Morgan.

She gasped, her dark eyes wide. Before he had time to say another word, she raced past him and out into the hallway, as if she'd seen the very devil himself.

Kyle didn't hesitate. He jumped out of his chair and ran after her.

Joanna Morgan raced down the hallway and ducked into a nearby ladies' room. She leaned against the door with all her weight, almost afraid he might barge in after her.

It couldn't be him. She wasn't supposed to ever see him again!

What was he doing here?

She waited a moment for her breathing to slow, then moved away from the door and stood at one of the three sinks. She stared into the mirror at her reflection. She looked as if she'd just seen a ghost. She had. She'd seen the ghost of passion past.

Kyle Ramsey. It had been him. There was no pretending. Kyle had been sitting in the ambassador's waiting room.

She closed her eyes and instantly was granted a vivid mental picture of him. That thick, wavy brown hair, those charcoal-gray eyes and those full, sensual lips had haunted her for the past couple of months.

It was almost exactly three months ago that she had made love to a virtual stranger. She'd like to believe that she had been drunk, but she knew better. Joanna never did anything to excess, especially drink.

No, she hadn't been drunk—she'd been intoxicated by the sexy charm that had radiated from his eyes, inebriated by the flirtatious, playful banter they had shared, smashed on the blatant masculine sexuality that had rolled off him in waves.

"Marie." A rapid knock sounded on the door.

She bit her lower lip, fighting against a wave of nausea. She'd never expected to see him again. Their night together had been a crazy lapse of judgment, a momentary slide into insanity, a wild ride of abandonment that had been completely out of character for her.

"Marie…Joanna." This time the knock was louder and echoed with a touch of impatience. "You can't stay in there all day. Sooner or later you have to come out."

He was right, of course. She couldn't stay in here forever, but she needed a little time to regain her equilibrium. She wasn't ready to come out yet. She still hadn't fully recovered from the absolute shock of seeing him again.

"Joanna, we have work to do." His voice came softly through the door.

Work to do? What work could they have to do?

A new wave of despair swept through her as her brain struggled to make sense of his words.

Oh heavens, he'd come from the ambassador's office. He'd been in there when the ambassador was to meet with the top gun navy pilot who was sharing her new assignment with her.

Just that morning Ambassador Templeton had told her about her new, important assignment—providing ground support for a team of top gun fliers who were coming in unofficially to patrol the skies over Montebello.

Kyle was the top gun navy pilot, and she would be working with him until the current tensions between Montebello and Tamir were resolved. Fate had a hysterical sense of humor, she thought. Unfortunately, at the moment she wasn't laughing, she simply felt as if she might throw up.

"Buck up," she commanded herself. "You're a professional and you will act like one." She slid a hand down her navy skirt, then drew a deep breath, opened the door and stepped out.

The last time she'd seen Kyle Ramsey, he'd been wearing jeans and a polo shirt. Well, that wasn't exactly true. The very last time she'd seen him, he'd been gloriously naked and asleep. That final vision of him exploded in her head, granting her an unwelcome image of his naked body stretched out on white sheets.

"Joanna M. Morgan." His gaze lingered a moment on her badge before returning to her face. "I assume the *M* stands for Marie?"

She nodded. He'd looked marvelous clad in jeans

and a shirt. He'd looked sinfully sexy naked against crisp white sheets, but at the moment he looked arrogant and commanding in his pristine, wrinkle-free uniform.

"So, should I call you Joanna or Marie?" His slate eyes glittered brightly. "Or is Marie the name you use only when you're picking up men in bars?"

She gasped. "I did not pick you up," she exclaimed indignantly before abruptly changing the subject. She fumbled with her purse and withdrew her car keys. "I understand I'm to take you to where you will be staying. Shall we go?"

She marched ahead of him, mortified by the entire situation. She'd allowed herself to be seduced, had indulged in some seduction of her own that night. But when she'd awakened early the next morning, she'd been appalled by what she'd done.

Even worse was discovering that Kyle Ramsey was in the military. She'd crept out of the room, consoling herself with the knowledge that she would never see him again.

She didn't look at him now until they were alone in the elevator. Then it was impossible to avoid doing so.

He filled the entire cubicle with his presence, with the spicy scent of his cologne and a subtle underlying fragrance of clean male. His eyes, with their sinful, long dark lashes and wicked gleam, swept her from head to toe, evoking tiny heat bursts wherever his gaze lingered.

His lips curved into a lazy smile that she remembered far too vividly from their night together.

"Don't you know it's the height of bad manners to sneak away from a lover while he's sleeping?"

"We weren't lovers and I think it's most unchivalrous of you to even mention that night."

He took a step closer to her. With the high beam of his bedroom eyes on her and the nearly blinding charm of his smile, she suddenly remembered how easy it had been to succumb to his seduction.

"We were lovers for that night, and why shouldn't I mention it? It's definitely a fond memory for me."

The elevator doors slid open, and Joanna nearly leaped out in an effort to escape the close proximity.

"Lieutenant Commander—"

"Kyle," he interjected as he fell into step beside her. "I figure any woman who has seen me naked should be able to call me by my first name."

Joanna refused to rise to his obvious baiting, but her cheeks burned with embarrassment. "Okay, fine," she continued as they left the embassy building and walked toward the nearby parking area. "Kyle, we have a job to do…an important job. And it would be best if we could just pretend that we met for the first time right now."

She stopped walking as they reached her small sports car. She unlocked the passenger door, then turned to face him, swallowing a gasp as she realized just how close he stood to her.

"Don't tell me you're married," he said.

"Of course not," she replied indignantly.

"Why didn't you tell me you worked at the embassy?" he asked, and took another step closer, effectively trapping her between her car and his hard, muscled body.

"Why didn't you tell me you were a hotshot top gun?" she countered.

She'd realized he was a military man early the next morning, when she'd awakened and gotten up to go to the bathroom. She'd spied his wallet on the bathroom counter. The wallet was open, displaying military identification. It was that that had prompted her to leave him, sneaking out like a thief just as the dawn had began to creep across the sky.

A slow, seductive smile curved his lips. "I didn't tell you I was a pilot because I wanted you to like me for who I was, not what I did for a living." He reached up and tucked an errant strand of hair behind her ear.

The simple touch galvanized her. She slid sideways, freeing herself from contact with the car and with him. "Like I said, it would be best if we'd just forget we had any dealings with each other before now."

She didn't wait for him to reply, but instead walked around the car and unlocked the driver's door. She slid behind the wheel at the same time he got in on the passenger side. She started to put the key in the ignition, but was stopped by his hand grabbing hers.

His long fingers curled around her wrist, warm and strong, and for just a second she remembered what those fingers had felt like touching her intimately. She felt a renewed burst of heat flame in her cheeks.

"Okay, we'll pretend that night never happened…on one condition," he said.

"What condition?" She eyed him suspiciously.

There was no humor in his eyes, no flirtatious light whatsoever. "Tell me why you left that morning. Tell me why you left without saying a word to me."

She pulled her hand from his, her mind racing for an explanation that would effectively douse any attraction he might still entertain for her.

"To be perfectly honest, Kyle," she began, wondering if perhaps what she was about to say was too over the top, verging on cruel. She quickly decided to forge ahead.

Better he hate her and stay out of her life than find out that their night of passion hadn't been without consequence. Better he hate her than find out she was pregnant with his child. "As lovers go, you weren't that great. In fact, you were terrible."

Chapter 2

Kyle stared at her for a long moment, then, unable to help himself, he threw back his head and laughed. "Darling, there are only two things in this world I've been told I do really well. One of them is flying planes..." he paused a moment, then continued "...and the other is making love."

He watched her cheeks burn with color as she jabbed the key into the ignition and started the engine. "You certainly weren't doing much complaining that night," he added softly. "And don't try to tell me you were pretending. I know the difference between reality and a good acting stint. I still remember the way your heart raced with mine, the sweet sound of your moans..."

"Okay," she snapped. "Forget I said anything." She threw the car into gear and backed out of the parking space. "Where am I taking you?"

"You know where Ramsey Enterprises is?"

Those sooty eyes of hers shot him a sharp glance. "You're one of those Ramseys?"

"Firstborn son." He was pleased his voice held none of his ambiguous feelings concerning his family, more specifically, his father. "There's a small apartment complex on the grounds of the business. My family has an apartment there, and that's where I'll be staying for the duration of this mission."

For a few minutes they rode in silence. Her scent, that mysterious, spicy fragrance that had haunted him, filled the confines of the small car and evoked heated memories of that night they'd spent together.

She could lie all she wanted about him being a lousy lover, but he had intimate knowledge of just how intensely she had responded to him.

They had made love as if all the time in eternity was theirs, and he had made certain that she was completely, almost exhaustively sated before he'd allowed himself the ultimate release.

He gazed at her as she maneuvered the car through the midmorning traffic. She was as lovely—lovelier—than he remembered. Her dark hair had the sheen of satin, and her skin was smooth and unblemished.

She had killer eyes. Dark with thick, sooty lashes, they sparkled with life and the promise of hidden passion...passion he'd tapped into and tasted and thoroughly enjoyed. They also held just a touch of mystery, prompting a man to want to delve inside her and discover all the secrets she might possess.

The night he had met her, the white dress she'd

been wearing had been short, exposing the length of her shapely legs, and tight, emphasizing her curves. She'd looked ultrafeminine, with red lipstick on her sensuous lips and a flirtatious glint in her eyes.

There was no sign of that woman in the one who now sat next to him. Clad in a navy blazer and skirt, with her hair pulled back and minimal makeup, she looked crisp, controlled and utterly professional.

"You didn't answer when I asked before—why didn't you tell me when I first met you that you worked for the embassy?" he asked.

"I wanted you to like me for who I was, not what I did." She echoed his own words back to him.

"Touché," he replied dryly. "At least I gave you my real name." There was more than a touch of irritation in his voice. And he was surprised to realize he was irritated with her…irritated that she'd given him a fake name.

He was miffed that she'd disappeared like a puff of smoke when he'd believed they had made a connection that had somehow transcended their explosive lovemaking.

There had been times when he'd wanted to vamoose from a bed before his companion awakened and he had to face the morning reality. But he'd never, ever had a woman hightail it out of his bed without a backward glance.

Until Joanna Marie Morgan.

"So, why didn't you give me your real name?" he asked.

"Don't you think we have more important things to discuss besides a foolish night spent three months ago?'' Although her voice was cool, her cheeks were still a becoming, unnatural pink.

"You're absolutely right," he said, peeved that she was reminding him of duty when that should be the first thing on his mind. He stared out the window at the passing scenery, then continued, "I'm assuming the ambassador filled you in on everything."

She nodded and made a righthand turn. "I believe I've been briefed on everything I need to know. I've already been in touch with the brass at the base, and they are expecting us to set up operations there sometime early in the morning. Unofficially, they will do whatever they can. Your team of fliers have been contacted and should all be here in Montebello by this evening."

He stared out the window for another long moment, then turned to look at her once again. "Do you really think Sheik Ahmed Kamal is going to order aggressive action against Montebello?"

She frowned. "I don't think anyone can guess what a man might do out of grief." She pulled into the entrance of Ramsey Enterprises and looked at him curiously as they came to a fork in the road.

He pointed to the left and she made the turn. "Sheik Ahmed is a strong, proud man," she continued, "a family man who suddenly finds his eldest son missing and suspects that King Marcus had something to do with his disappearance. King Marcus is also functioning from grief and anger from the loss of his own son, Prince Lucas, who reportedly perished in a plane crash a few months ago. At the moment, I'd say one is as much a loose cannon as the other.''

"And a loose cannon is exactly what this area of the world doesn't need."

"Exactly," she agreed.

"Pull up in front of the apartment building," he said, pointing ahead to the attractive three-story structure. "Our family quarters are on the top floor. You can just let me off in front." He offered her a lazy smile. "Unless you would like to come up and have a replay of our night together."

She braked so hard that, had he not been wearing his seat belt, he would have been catapulted out the front window. When she turned to look at him, her eyes were dark fires of anger and her cheeks were stained with color.

"That night, Kyle, was an anomaly. I acted completely out of character and I regret that it even happened. I have been assigned to work with you, and that's what I intend to do—work and nothing more." Her eyes pleaded with him. "Can't you just forget about it?"

His desire to touch her was overwhelming. A simple caress to her soft cheek, or a stroke of that silky, shiny hair—that's all he wanted. It was as if he needed a physical confirmation that she was real and not some mirage that would once again vanish in the blink of an eye.

This irrational need to touch her simply renewed his irritation with her once again. He opened the car door and stepped out, then opened the back door to retrieve his duffel bag. "Why don't you come by for me tomorrow at 0500 hours. I can have my men in the air by dawn.''

''Fine. I'll see you in the morning.''

He slammed the door and jumped back as she pulled away, roaring off as if all the demons from hell were chasing her. He watched until her car was out of sight, then turned and headed into the apartment building.

Emotions rolled inside him, unsettling emotions about Joanna. He'd spent three months thinking about her, thinking about that night they'd shared. Of all the women he'd been with, the image of her had remained in his head longer than any other.

Was it because she was the only one who had ever walked away from him? Was it because in his past relationships, long and short, he had been the one who had always walked away?

He nodded to the security man on duty, then headed for the elevator that would take him to the top floor apartment.

As soon as the elevator began moving upward, he felt an old familiar constriction tightening his chest.

When the elevator stopped, he stepped out and dug in his pocket for the key to the door just ahead. He opened the door and stepped onto the plush, thick beige carpeting. The air was comfortably cool and smelled faintly of lemon oil and fresh flowers.

His mother must have called in the cleaning crew to make sure the place was ready for his arrival, despite the fact that he'd told her he'd probably be staying at the base.

He hated staying here, much preferred the simple,

impersonal space at the military base. This luxurious, four-bedroom apartment, which spanned the entire top floor of the building, was a testimony that his fat-cat father had sold out long ago and chosen money over honor.

Kyle dropped his duffel bag on the floor next to the overstuffed sofa, then walked over to the marble bar that occupied a corner of the living room.

What he wanted was a drink—a smooth shot of good whiskey to take the edge off the tremendous shock of seeing Marie…Joanna…again. Instead, he reached for a can of fruit juice, knowing he needed to be clearheaded early in the morning.

He popped the lid, took a swallow, then sank down on the sofa. Joanna's drink of choice had been a Tom Collins with a lime twist, and when he'd kissed her for the first time, he'd tasted not only the intense heat of her mouth, but a touch of gin and a tang of lime as well.

Funny, now that he thought about the conversation they'd shared that night, he realized it had been pretty superficial.

They hadn't talked about their jobs or their families, they'd merely indulged in a lighthearted banter-ing that had been both amusing and stimulating. Their conversation had been filled with innuendos, a verbal foreplay he had found exciting.

But beneath the superficiality, he'd sensed some-thing in her that had touched something inside him…a wistfulness, a yearning…something he couldn't quite define and couldn't quite forget. All he knew was that he had been incredibly drawn to her and had believed she'd felt the same way about him.

In the months since that night, she had grown to epic proportions in his mind. Was she simply a player? A woman who took her pleasure with men, then fled so there would be no messy emotions, no unnecessary entanglements?

After the initial shock of seeing him today, she'd seemed fairly cool and calm. Her desire that he forget their night together hit a sour note with him.

Had she been totally unaffected by what they had shared? Could she so easily forget how sweetly their bodies had come together? Could she dismiss without pause the magic they'd spun when dancing together, laughing together, loving together? He frowned with annoyance. It would seem so.

He finished his juice and threw out the can, then picked up his duffel bag and headed into the bedroom he called his own when staying at the apartment. The room, like the rest of the place, was large and luxurious. Decorated in deep blues and pale silver, it boasted big, masculine furniture. Photos of Kyle in uniform hung on the walls.

It took him only minutes to hang his clothes in the closet and set his toiletries on the counter in the adjoining bathroom. Then he wandered back into the living room, his head still consumed with thoughts of Joanna Marie Morgan.

She had made it quite clear that she had no intention of picking up where they'd left off, that she just wanted to forget that single night they had shared together.

But he couldn't do that. He had to have some answers. He needed to have some closure where she was concerned. He wanted to know why she had left him that morning after they had made love so passionately, then fallen asleep in one another's arms.

More than answers, he wanted one more night with her. What he wasn't sure of was if he wanted one more night of the pleasure of making love to her, or if he simply wanted an opportunity to be the one to walk away.

At precisely 0500 hours the next morning, Joanna knocked on the Ramsey apartment door. The security officer on duty had told her to go on up, that Lieutenant Commander Ramsey was waiting for her. For the past month she'd been experiencing morning nausea, but none quite as intense as what she felt at the moment.

Nerves, she told herself. She'd been a nervous wreck from the moment she'd seen him again. The one time in her life she'd made a mistake and done something irrational, spontaneous and stupid, fate had to be a perverse jokester and throw the mistake right back in her face.

Her "mistake" opened the door, looking as breathtakingly handsome and male as ever. "Ah, Joanna, right on time." He stepped aside and gestured her in.

She swept past him, knowing he was freshly showered from the scent of soap. He was dressed not in his uniform, but casually, in tight jeans and a pale blue, short-sleeved dress shirt that emphasized taut biceps. It was similar to what he'd been wearing on the night they had first met.

He closed the door behind her and she found herself in a huge, airy living room. "There's coffee in the kitchen. Help yourself."

"No, thanks," she replied, the very thought making her stomach twist and buck. Lately it was rare that she drank coffee or ate anything besides crackers before noon. Her morning sickness made it virtually impossible to keep much of anything down.

"Then have a seat. I'll be ready to head out in just a minute." He disappeared down a hallway and into what she assumed was one of the bedrooms.

Joanna didn't sit, but rather wandered around the room. At least he'd been impersonal and businesslike so far, she thought as she moved to a wall of windows and peered out.

It was still too dark outside to be able to see what kind of view the windows would provide. In her mind, she didn't see the darkness of predawn, but rather a vivid picture of how Kyle had looked the morning she'd sneaked out of the hotel room.

He'd been gloriously naked and stretched out on his stomach. His golden, tanned back had looked impossibly broad against the white sheets of the bed, and his slender waist, buttocks and long, lanky legs had made him look like a model in a pinup calendar.

From the moment he'd walked into that bar that night and their eyes had met, she'd known. She'd known that before the night was over they would be in bed together. It had been wonderfully exciting and more than a little bit frightening at the same time.

She moved away from the window and consciously forced herself to focus on a bookcase and an array of framed photographs on one of the shelves.

They were apparently photos of the Ramsey family. In one picture, a smiling older couple stood just behind three young boys. It was obvious the child in the center was Kyle. Even then, at the age of about ten or twelve, he'd been handsome. His features were clean-cut and well defined, and there was already a confident gleam in his eyes.

She assumed the older couple were his parents, and it was obvious by the expressions on their faces that they were proud of their boys.

A wistful yearning echoed in an empty chamber of her heart. How wonderful it must be to have a family, to always know you had a place where you belonged, where you were loved.

"I see you found the family photos."

She whirled around to face him. "Yes. These are your brothers?" She pointed to the photo that had captured her attention.

"Yeah." Kyle walked over and stood next to her…far too close. "This is Jake. He's twenty-nine, two years younger than I am. He just became CEO of Ramsey Enterprises." He pointed to the other young boy in the picture. "And that's Tyler. He's twenty-eight and works for the company, also."

"So, you're the only rebel who didn't go to work for Ramsey Enterprises?" she asked, half-teasingly.

His eyes darkened and he turned away from the pictures. "Something like that."

She looked at one of the other pictures. It was an older photograph of a young man in uniform. "Your father was in the Air Force?"

"Yeah. He's a decorated Vietnam War hero." Pride was evident in his low voice. For a moment his gaze remained on the picture of his father, then he frowned. "But he quit the military to join corporate America and fill his coffers with money." He turned to look at her, his gray eyes turbulent. "Let's get going."

"Okay." She'd obviously touched a nerve.

As they left the apartment and got into her car, Joanna thought of everything she knew about Ramsey Enterprises. She knew that the company was owned by Edward Ramsey and headquartered in the United States. The plant on Montebello was one of three that worked to produce plane parts.

She hadn't imagined the tension in Kyle's voice when he'd spoken of his father. Apparently there was strain between Edward Ramsey and his firstborn son.

"So, what about your family? You have brothers or sisters?" he asked when they were in her car and headed toward the nearby military base.

The yearning that never seemed to be completely still echoed once again inside her. "No brothers, no sisters. No immediate family since my father died three years ago."

"What about your mother?" he asked.

"She died when I was born."

"That's tough."

Joanna said nothing, although she wanted to tell

him that the loss of her mother hadn't been half as tough as life with her military father.

She'd spent her childhood being pulled from base to base and raised by hired help, some good, some not so good, and none of them family.

The end result was that she had no place to call home...no connection to anyone else in the world. The night she had met Kyle and slept with him, she had been driven by an overwhelming need to connect, and ''connecting'' with him had been frighteningly wonderful—until she'd realized he was military, just like her father.

''That night I first met you, I just assumed you were a local woman. Your coloring—your features—are of the locals.''

She felt his gaze warming her face and wondered why, despite knowing he was absolutely wrong for her and there would never, ever be any future relationship between them, she remained so acutely aware of him, so intimately drawn to him.

''My mother was a native of Montebello. My father met her while he was based here.''

''Your father was in the military?''

''Army.'' She offered nothing else and searched her mind for a way to change the topic. ''I understand there are ten pilots comprising your team for this mission.''

He nodded and directed his gaze forward out the window, where the military base had come into view. ''Two of the men will aid you in ground support, the rest of us will take eight-hour shifts in the air, with time on the ground only for refueling. We'll refuel in shifts as well, so there is always at least one plane flying.''

They stopped speaking as she pulled up to the guard shack in front of the military base. Fifteen minutes later, she sat in the back of a small room that had been transformed into an operation center for their ''unofficial'' mission. State-of-the-art equipment lined one wall, complete with radar screens and high-tech computers.

She watched and listened as Kyle addressed the men seated before him, explaining what their jobs would be and the shifts that would be taken.

It was impossible not to notice the authority and respect Kyle commanded from the men. He wore his casual clothes as elegantly as he wore his uniform, and an appealing self-confidence oozed from his very pores.

He's the father of my baby. The realization struck her like a startling blow to the chest. Until this moment, the baby inside her had been something of a dream, not quite real to her. But now the reality exploded inside her.

She was pregnant, and in approximately six months time she would have a baby—Kyle's baby. Her hand moved to her abdomen, as if to stroke the life that grew within.

The child she carried would get half of its DNA from the man before her. And Kyle had no idea that on the night they had shared, he'd given her a piece of himself that could never be retrieved, a piece that would be a part of her life for the rest of her days.

What would he do if he knew? There was no way

she could guess what his reaction would be if he discovered that he was the father of the baby.

She knew how he kissed, how his skin felt beneath her fingertips. She knew how his heart felt racing against her own, how his breathing quickened with each stroke of her skin. But all of that intimate knowledge told her nothing about how he might react to the news of his pending fatherhood.

Not that she intended to tell him. No way! Again her hand touched her stomach and a maelstrom of love cascaded through her. This was her baby, and the child would be the family she never had.

She knew all she needed to know about Kyle Ramsey. He was first and foremost a military man, a rootless bachelor who thrived on adventure, a man who probably had a woman in every port.

Kyle was a man just like her father, who had pulled her from post to post, never staying in one place long enough for her to feel any stability or sense of home. All he'd wanted to do was fight wars. He didn't want a family or roots.

For a single night she'd been Kyle's Montebello woman, and if she'd slept later that morning, she was certain she would have been the one to wake up all alone in bed.

She knew from experience that it was better to have no father than a military father. Kyle Ramsey would never know about the baby. Never.

Chapter 3

"Eagle One to base."

Joanna swallowed the yawn that had been about to take control of her mouth, and flipped the button on the radio control panel so she could respond. "Base... Go ahead, Eagle One."

"Ah, McCreary must have taken a break." Kyle's voice was deep and smooth and sounded as if he were standing right next to her instead of thousands of feet in the air. "Your sweet, sexy voice is a pleasant surprise."

Heat swept through Joanna. Drat the man, even from miles away he could set her heart to racing. What was it about him that made her feel all fluttery inside? Maybe she had indigestion.

"Just thought I'd let you know we're coming in," he continued. "The relief team just came into sight."

"The ground crew is ready for you, and you're cleared for landing," she replied, and smiled at Jason McCreary as he resumed a seat next to her and put on a second headset. Jason was an old friend of Kyle's and a top-notch flyer who had been assigned to ground support with Joanna for the day.

"Joanna." Kyle's voice came again, strong and clear over the radio. "That morning you left me in bed all alone in the hotel room...was it because I was hogging all the pillows?"

Joanna couldn't hide her gasp of disbelief that he would ask such a thing over the radio with McCreary sitting right next to her. "Eagle One, you're breaking up. I can't understand you. You're cleared for landing."

She yanked off the headset, aware of McCreary's amused gaze on her. She turned and glared at him. "Don't you say a word."

He held up his hands and grinned, his freckles appearing to dance all across his broad, open face. "I wasn't *going* to say a word," he protested, his blue eyes twinkling merrily. "Of course, I'd be lying to you if I didn't say I wasn't just a tad curious."

Joanna got up from her chair. "You know what curiosity did to the cat," she replied.

He laughed and focused his attention back on business as one of the other pilots radioed in.

Joanna had quickly taken a liking to Jason McCreary, whose round face and freckles made him look like an old version of the irrepressible Huck Finn. He was friendly and open and spent much of the day talking about his wife and his two kids, whom he obviously adored. Joanna had been totally at ease around him.

However, she had certainly not intended for him to know that she'd spent any time at all in a hotel room with his commanding officer.

Drat Kyle Ramsey, anyway. The man was beyond aggravating.

She fumed inwardly and poured herself a cup of water from the nearby cooler. Sitting in one of the chairs that surrounded a large table, she gazed at her watch. It was almost three o'clock.

The first day of their mission had zoomed by despite the fact that it had been a relatively boring one. Boring was what they wanted. Boring meant there had been no signs of aggression from Tamir, no lives at risk or crazy aerial combat dramas.

She sipped the water and realized she was ravenous. She'd eaten no breakfast, had consumed only an apple and a small bag of pretzels around eleven, and now her stomach was letting her know it required a real meal.

Officially, her duties were over for the day, and the way the schedule was set up, she wasn't required to be back here until two the next afternoon. She pulled out one of the schedules from her paperwork and studied it.

It annoyed her that Kyle had set up the work schedule and had arranged for her to work all the same times he was. As he'd handed her the schedule, he'd mentioned that this way they could ride to and from the base together. As if he didn't have access to other transportation. As if he couldn't afford to rent a car...

She didn't understand what he hoped to gain by forcing them to spend time together. Surely she'd made it clear to him that she didn't intend to indulge in a repeat performance of the night they had spent together.

Although she'd be lying to herself if she didn't acknowledge that for the past twenty-four hours she'd spent far too much time remembering that night.

She had a feeling that the time she'd spent in Kyle's arms would always be a heady, powerful memory, that it was forever burned not only into her head, but into every fiber of her body.

She was still seated at the table when Kyle walked in. Instantly, as he entered through the door, the space in the room seemed to shrink and the air filled with crackling energy.

That had been one of the first things that drew her to him that night in the bar—the aura of intense energy that had emanated from him.

"Good afternoon," he said, his gray eyes glittering brightly as he grinned rakishly at Joanna. He walked past McCreary and ruffled the man's red hair. "Hey, McCreary, how's that woman of yours?"

"Great," McCreary replied as Kyle went to the cooler and got himself a glass of water.

It was obvious he was pumped with energy, and Joanna couldn't help but notice how utterly wonderful he looked in his flight suit. The navy material pulled taut across his broad shoulders and displayed his slim stomach and lean hips to perfection.

He downed the water, crumpled the paper cup and tossed it in the trash, then grinned once again at Joanna. "Our first patrol can be written down as a success. We encountered nothing but blue skies and a fantastic view of the wonders of Montebello. You ready to go?"

She nodded and stood.

"Just let me get out of these clothes," he said, and began to unzip the flight suit. Joanna's breath seemed to momentarily stop as she caught a glimpse of tanned chest and a sprinkling of dark hair before he turned and grabbed his clothes, then disappeared into the bathroom next door.

She released a sigh of relief, grateful he'd left when he had. She didn't want to see any more of that hard, muscled chest, didn't want to remember how that flesh, those muscles and that springy hair had felt beneath her fingertips.

And she certainly didn't want to remember the pleasure of her bare breasts against his chest. The man was positively a menace to her peace of mind.

He returned dressed in the clothes he'd had on when she'd picked him up that morning. "Ready?" he asked.

"See you tomorrow," McCreary said as Joanna grabbed her purse.

"Contact us if there are any developments or problems," Kyle said to McCreary.

As Joanna and Kyle walked to her car, Joanna fought the impulse to tear into him about the personal, intimate information he'd relayed over the radio, but she had a feeling he wanted to get a rise out of her. She decided her best course of action was not to snap at his bait.

"This island has got to be one of the most beautiful I've ever seen from the sky," he said as they got into her car. "The last time I was here, I never got an opportunity to do any sightseeing."

"So you haven't seen the beautiful beaches or the mountains."

"The only things I've seen while here are the military base, Ramsey Enterprises and a certain hotel room." He gazed at her meaningfully.

"Then you must find time to see the island," she said, once again refusing to rise to his obvious baiting.

"Perhaps I can persuade you to give me an island tour when we have a little extra time."

She smiled dryly and started her car. "Your powers of persuasion aren't that good."

He laughed, that wonderful deep rumble that seemed to resonate from his chest. "Could I persuade you to stop and get something to eat right now? I am absolutely starving."

The request seemed innocent enough, and she thought of several drive-through fast-food places she could hit on the way back to his apartment. She would get herself something as well; that way she wouldn't have to cook and could just go home and relax.

"All right," she agreed as they drove away from the base. "I'm pretty hungry myself."

"Great, I know a terrific little place not far from here that serves the best Mediterranean food."

Joanna frowned. "I was thinking more of something like a drive-through."

She felt his gaze warm on her face. "What's the matter, Joanna? Afraid of being seen with me in public?"

"Of course not," she scoffed, inwardly chiding herself for her uneasiness. How difficult could it be to sit across from him and eat a meal in a public restaurant? "Mediterranean sounds great to me."

"Good." He sat back in the seat and looked inordinately pleased with himself.

He gave her directions to the restaurant, one she'd never eaten at but had heard had excellent food. It took them only minutes to reach it.

The interior was dark and atmospheric, with small round tables set in tiny alcoves, allowing the utmost in intimacy.

Joanna's first impulse was to back out, to tell him to forget it, but the scents of savory food wafted in the air and again she told herself it was ridiculous to be worried about a simple meal shared with Kyle Ramsey.

There were just a few diners there. It was too late for the lunch crowd and far too early for the dinner rush. Joanna and Kyle were led to a table near the back of the restaurant, where the lighting was dim and the soft strains of exotic lute music could be heard drifting in the air.

They were handed menus, then left alone. Joanna

studied hers with determined concentration, far too aware of the man sitting across the table from her.

The table was so small that she knew if she stretched her legs out just a little bit, she would encounter the long, lanky length of his. She consciously kept her arms bent, the menu close to her chest, not wanting their hands to accidentally touch, or her arms to inadvertently brush his.

"If you wind yourself up any tighter, you might just disappear altogether."

She looked up to meet his teasing gray eyes. She relaxed her arms slightly and sighed. "It's…it's just been a long day."

"Any day I get to spend airborne is a terrific day."

She closed her menu, but kept it tight against her chest. "You love flying." It was a statement rather than a question.

He didn't get an opportunity to reply before the waiter appeared to take their orders. Joanna asked for a vegetable pita sandwich and a soft drink. Kyle ordered as if he hadn't eaten for months, starting with a salad, a hot appetizer and an entré of lamb chops.

He finished by asking for a bottle of wine. When the waiter took their menus, Joanna felt naked without the large laminated book to hide behind.

Kyle grinned at her as the waiter departed. "Flying always makes me hungry. It's like all of my senses go into overdrive. Food tastes better, scents smell better…" His gaze held hers intently. "Everything is more intense."

There was a power in those slate eyes, they held an intimate knowledge coupled with a touch of arrogance. It was impossible for her to look into his eyes and not remember that he knew every inch of her naked skin, had kissed and caressed her more intimately than anyone ever had in her life.

The waiter reappeared with the wine. "Would you like a glass?" Kyle asked, and raised the bottle to pour.

"No, thank you. None for me." Her head was dizzy enough without the additional effects of a glass of wine. Besides, even though the doctor had told her an occasional glass of wine was all right, she wasn't taking any chances with the baby.

"Would you prefer a mixed drink? A Tom Collins?"

It surprised her that he remembered what she'd been drinking the night they had met. "No thanks, I'm fine." She took a sip of her water and watched as he poured himself a glass of the wine.

He had nice hands—large and oddly graceful despite their masculinity. "So, you've always enjoyed flying?" She desperately grappled for a neutral topic of conversation.

He nodded. "Always. When I was a young boy, everything about flying and planes fascinated me. I had a collection of model airplanes that hung from my ceiling no matter where we were stationed. If I'd had my way, I'd have joined the navy and become a pilot when I was seventeen, but my father refused to sign for me."

"Why? Was it because he thought you were too young?"

Kyle paused a moment to take a sip of his wine.

"No. He wanted me to go to college, get a business degree and take over the reins of Ramsey Enterprises. So I went to college, got my degree, then joined the navy anyway."

Although his words came easily and without emotion, there was a new tension in his body that let her know this had been a source of great conflict between father and son.

"And you've never regretted your decision? Never wished you'd gone to work for Ramsey Enterprises?" she asked.

"Never. In fact, in less than a month my current tour of duty is over and I have every intention of reenlisting. Unlike my father, I have no desire to dabble in corporate America. I'm a career military man."

A career military man. Just as her father had been. Kyle's life would follow the same path as her father's had taken. He'd leave at a moment's notice, drop everything to fight wars in distant lands. And, like her father, his wars would be more important than his family.

His proud words merely confirmed to her what she had instinctively known after that single night with him—that there would never, ever be a future for the two of them. She had been absolutely right to sneak out and leave him sleeping in that hotel room.

Again the waiter interrupted their conversation, this time to deliver their meals. When he had once again left their table, Kyle leaned forward, his metal-flecked eyes gleaming with more than a touch of wickedness. "Was it because I snored?"

"I'm sorry, Eagle One, you're breaking up and I can't understand you."

He leaned back in his chair and laughed. Goodness, but she loved the sound of his laughter. His gaze lingered on her face, then swept slowly down, warming her breasts before returning to her face once again. "You are a piece of work, lady. You definitely intrigue me."

She forced an easy smile. "I think you wouldn't be half so intrigued if you awakened that morning and I'd been there asking you when I'd hear from you again, if you were going to call me, when we could get together." She leaned forward and met his gaze boldly. "I think you're intrigued simply because I ran out on you before you could run out on me."

Surprise lit his features, then he grinned once again, that lazy, sexy smile that shot heat through her. "Then we'll just have to see to it that the next time, neither of us runs."

"There is never going to be a next time," she replied.

His grin didn't waver, but his gaze once again swept the length of her. Hot...and intimate. She felt each and every place his gaze lingered. "Don't be so sure about that." He picked up his fork and focused his attention on his food.

Joanna picked up her soda and took a long drink, as if by drinking the cold liquid she could quell the fires he'd set burning inside her. There had been no threat in his words, but rather promise...the promise of being held in his arms once again, the promise of feeling his body intimately against her own.

She'd been worried about the fact that she was so acutely aware of him, but she suddenly realized that wasn't what she should be worried about.

The danger he posed to her wasn't so much due to the fact that he was an attractive, virile man, but rather that he made her so vividly aware of herself as a woman…a desirable woman.

All the men at the embassy looked at her as if she was asexual. They knew she was bright, that she could get the job done, that she was efficient and committed, but none of them seemed to see her as a young woman with dreams and needs. She was a machine as far as her co-workers were concerned, and there were times when she longed to be recognized simply as a woman.

Kyle was dangerous because he made her feel utterly feminine, winsomely beautiful and achingly desirable. He was dangerous to her because even though she was certain she did not want him in her life, there was a small part of her that wouldn't mind having him in her bed one last time.

Kyle was stimulated, both by his hours in the fighter plane and by the woman who sat across from him daintily eating her sandwich.

That she was intelligent was a given. She wouldn't be working in the embassy as a military attaché if she weren't extremely bright.

She was also beautiful, with a slender body that was both sexy and feminine. But it wasn't just her physical appeal that intrigued him, although he had to admit he was strongly attracted to her.

He was also drawn to her wit and surprised at how easily and astutely she'd seen into his thoughts and musings about the night they'd spent together.

And he wondered how right she was. If he'd been the one to disappear that morning, would he be as intrigued with her?

"You mentioned earlier that your mother was from Montebello. Do you still have family here?" he asked as they continued to eat.

She nodded. "A grandmother and an aunt and her children. That's what brought me back to Montebello when my father passed away. I wanted to be near what was left of my family." Joanna frowned, a trace of something he thought might be sadness darkening her eyes. Perhaps he was not the only one burdened by family conflicts.

"Where were you living before that?" he asked, wanting to change the subject, remove the shadows from her lovely eyes.

"Washington, D.C. I was working as an assistant to Senator Bolin."

"Quite a different pace here on Montebello than in Washington," Kyle observed.

She nodded, her hair a shiny waterfall escaping the plain brown barrette at the nape of her neck. His fingers itched to release the clasp, allow all the strands to fall free. "But I have to say, the pace here has changed. Tensions are much higher now, especially since the recent bombing."

"Yeah, I heard about the bomb, but haven't heard

all the details.'' Kyle frowned, the loveliness of her
hair momentarily forgotten.

''It was about a month ago. The bomb exploded
in a civilian square. It completely destroyed a restaurant and trapped people inside the rubble. People
died in the blast.'' Once again her eyes were dark
and troubled.

''I read in one of the newspapers that nobody has
been found responsible yet for the bombing.''

She shook her head. ''That's true, however King
Marcus is certain that Sheik Ahmed is responsible
for the bomb. Sheik Ahmed, of course, denies any
involvement, but the whole thing has made tensions
so much higher. And it has made the people of Montebello afraid.''

''There is nothing more frightening than the threat
of a bomb.''

''Bombs are so indiscriminate in taking victims,''
she replied. She looked down at her half-eaten sandwich, as if she'd lost her appetite because of the seriousness of their discussion.

''We got a little heavy here, didn't we,'' he said,
wanting to see her smile again. She had a smile that
warmed him to the pit of his stomach. ''How about
you tell me what you like to do in your spare time.''

She shrugged and used her fork to toy with the
last bit of her sandwich. ''I don't get a lot of spare
time. I work pretty long hours, and lately often six
or seven days a week. But when I do get a little spare
time, I enjoy going to the beach. I like to read and
do crossword puzzles and I enjoy watching old mov-

ies." Her sensual lips moved into a wry smile. "I lead a very boring, quiet life, Kyle."

"Unless you're dancing in a bar after having indulged in several Tom Collinses," he teased.

He loved watching her blush, and she didn't disappoint him. Red stains appeared on her cheeks. "I told you, that night was completely out of character for me. That was the first time I'd been in that club and in that hotel."

"So, what exactly made you act so out of character that night?" Although he kept his tone light and teasing, he genuinely wanted to know the answer.

She looked down at her plate, a thoughtful frown creasing her forehead. When she looked back up at him, the frown was gone. "Let's just say I'd had an unusually rough day and decided to kick up my heels a little."

He had a feeling it was much more than that, that there were a hundred things she was not confiding to him, and his interest in her only increased.

For the first time that he could ever remember he was as eager to get into a woman's head as he was to get her into his bed. And for the first time in his life, he wasn't sure of the odds of accomplishing either.

Chapter 4

The ringing telephone startled Kyle from a deep sleep. He shot up in the bed and quickly grabbed the nearby receiver, adrenaline pumping. His first impulse was to expect trouble. Had a plane encountered problems? Had Tamir made a move? Had one of his men gone down?

"Yes?" he barked into the phone.

"Kyle? Darling, is that you?"

The adrenaline drained out of him and he flopped back on the bed at the sound of his mother's familiar voice. "Yeah, Mom, it's me."

"Oh dear, I woke you, didn't I? I'm sorry. It's almost bedtime here so it must be just after noon there. I assumed you'd either be at work or awake."

"I've got a crazy schedule at the moment. I'm working all hours of the day and night." Kyle looked at the clock on the nightstand and saw that it was just after one. He wasn't due at the base until eleven that night. "What's up?"

"Does something have to be up for me to want to hear my eldest son's voice?"

Kyle smiled as a vision of his mother filled his mind. Beatrice Ramsey had always been a stay-at-home mom. She'd raised her three sons with discipline, love and a sense of humor. There was no woman on earth Kyle loved and respected more than his mother. "It's good to hear your voice, too, Mom."

"Are you taking care of yourself? Eating proper meals and getting your rest?"

His smile widened. Even though he was thirty-one years old, his mother still worried about him as if he were ten. "Don't worry. I'm taking good care of myself."

"If you had a wife, I wouldn't worry so much about you."

"Don't start," Kyle exclaimed, unwilling to be a recipient of one of his mother's frequent lectures on the joys of marriage. Something must have happened recently for her to even begin one of her lectures.

"Sandy Dennison just had her third grandbaby yesterday," Beatrice continued. *Bingo,* Kyle thought. The incident that had prompted this phone call extolling the pleasures of married life. "Three grandbabies, and her son is two years younger than you."

"Mom, you know that isn't what I want for myself," he chided softly. It wasn't as if they hadn't had this conversation before.

Beatrice sighed, the long-suffering sigh Kyle suspected every mother in the world had down to perfection. "I can hope, can't I?"

"You'd do better to aim your hopes toward Jake and Tyler. The odds of them giving you a daughter-in-law and a grandchild are much better than me."

"I don't know what's wrong with you boys that none of you has found a wonderful, loving woman yet. I'll probably be in my grave before one of you finally gives me a grandbaby to love and to spoil."

Kyle wisely didn't reply.

"Well, dear, your father wants to talk with you. I'll put him on."

Instantly, tension filled Kyle. Conversations with his father were difficult for him, especially lately. There was a tiny part of Kyle that believed he was a major disappointment to his dad, that Edward Ramsey had never really forgiven him for his decision not to work for Ramsey Enterprises.

"Kyle." His father's deep voice boomed across the line.

"Hi, Dad." Kyle swung his legs over the side of the bed and stood. For some reason he felt as if he needed to be on his feet to speak to his father.

"How are things in Montebello?"

"Fine. Everything is just fine."

"I heard you tell your mother you're working a lot. Anything interesting going on?"

Kyle heard the unspoken questions in his father's voice. The old man wanted to know what sort of mission Kyle was on, but Edward had lost his right to know about military missions when he'd turned his back on the armed forces and joined the race for bucks.

"Just the same old, same old," Kyle replied.

There was a moment of silence between father and son, a weighty silence that raised Kyle's tension several notches. "Kyle, I have a favor to ask you," his father finally said.

"What kind of a favor?"

"I know your tour is up in a couple of weeks, and before you do anything about that, I'd like to have an opportunity to sit down face-to-face and talk to you."

"About what? Dad, we've been through this a million times," Kyle began. The last thing he wanted was a sit-down discussion with his father that would only make Kyle feel guilty about the path he'd chosen in his life.

"Kyle, please. I'm just asking you to hold off making any decisions until we can talk. I should be able to get to Montebello in the next week or so. All I'm asking is that you wait until after that to re-enlist."

"All right, I can do that," Kyle replied, already dreading the conversation they would eventually have and certain that it would be nothing but a rehash of their collision of dreams.

After saying goodbye to his father moments later, Kyle paced the living room restlessly. He didn't have to be back at the base till late that night and he'd planned on sleeping most of the day. However, the conversation with his dad had chased any sleepiness away.

He wandered over to the bookcase and stared at the various photos that lined the shelves. There was several of his father in his Air Force uniform.

When Kyle was growing up, his father had been his hero. Edward Ramsey had been doing what Kyle wanted to do, dreamed of doing—flying planes. And for much of his childhood, Kyle hoped to grow up to be just like his father.

Then, when Kyle was fourteen, his father had quit the military and sold out. He'd traded his country's uniform for a business suit, and exchanged jet engines for power lunches. It had been at that moment that Kyle and his relationship had undergone a drastic change.

For years Kyle had heard his dad talk about the honor and duty of serving his country. Then, in what felt to Kyle to be a split-second decision, Edward Ramsey had been seduced by the corporate world.

To say that Edward Ramsey had been successful was an understatement. Not only did the Ramsey family have oil interests all over the world, but Ramsey Enterprises was a multimillion-dollar industry. His father had taken his contacts and the friendships he'd developed while serving his country and turned them to personal profit.

Kyle knew what his dad wanted to discuss with him. He wanted to plead one more time for Kyle to turn his back on his military career and go into the family business. It was to be a rehash of the same argument they'd been having for years.

Kyle made himself a late lunch, then napped on the sofa, but by nine that evening he thought he might go mad if he had to spend another minute in the confines of the family apartment. He'd showered and done a load of laundry, and could find nothing else to do to waste time. On impulse he picked up the phone and dialed Joanna's residence.

In the four days they had been working together, he hadn't called her at home, although he'd thought about it more than once.

"Hello?"

Her voice was lower than normal and had the fuzzy edges of sleepiness. Instantly Kyle was tormented with a picture of her in bed. He knew exactly what she'd look like—her hair all tousled and her dark eyes slightly glazed. Her body would be toasty warm beneath the rumpled sheets.

He shook his head to dispel the evocative image. "Joanna...it's me."

"Kyle, what's wrong?" Instantly any trace of sleepiness was gone from her voice.

"Relax, nothing is wrong," he assured her. "I was just wondering if it would be possible for us to get to the base a little early."

"Of course. Just tell me when." As she spoke he heard the faint rustle of material and realized she must be getting out of bed.

"As soon as possible," he replied, again gifted with a mental picture that sent his blood pressure several degrees higher. Did she sleep naked or in a nightgown? She had slept naked the night they had spent together. That night he'd been her gown, draping her with his warmth, covering her nakedness with his body.

"I can be there in about thirty minutes," she said.

"I'll be ready." They said their goodbyes and he hung up. Where before his head had been filled with thoughts of his father, now it was consumed with thoughts of Joanna.

The past few days spent in her company had only managed to make him hungrier for her. While he was in the air flying, her sexy voice taunted him with professional details. When he was on the ground and in her company, his body reacted like an adolescent boy's, flushing with heat and pumping with desire.

He alternated between being fascinated and irritated with her...irritated with his own crazy fascination. Never, ever had a woman plagued his thoughts like she did, and he found that both intoxicating and aggravating.

That he wanted her again was a given. The memory of their night together was not enough to sustain him for the rest of his life. He needed—wanted—another night with her, to make love to her one more time.

Maybe if he did he could finally, irrevocably, get her out of his system. At least that's what he hoped would happen.

Exactly thirty minutes after he'd hung up, she arrived to pick him up. As soon as he got into her car, he smelled the scent of her...fresh, clean, as if she'd just stepped out of the shower. Mingling with the refreshing scent was the evocative whisper of her spicy, mysterious perfume.

"I'm sorry, Kyle, but I left my place so fast, I left the log there. Do you mind if we stop back there so

I can grab it?'' she asked as soon as he climbed into the passenger seat.

"Not at all. We have plenty of time before we are officially on duty.'' He settled back in the seat and fastened his seat belt. "Besides, this way you can show me where you live.''

She cast him a quick glance. "Why would you want to see where I live?''

"Curiosity,'' he answered truthfully. "I think you can glean personality clues about people by seeing where and how they choose to live.''

"Really?'' she said, obviously amused. "And tell me, Kyle, where do you live?''

"Mostly in military housing or hotel rooms.''

She nodded, a knowing smile curving her lips.

"What?'' he asked. "According to my theory, that makes me unencumbered, free and independent.''

"According to your theory that makes you most likely devoid of personality, rootless and afraid to make commitments,'' she countered.

He laughed, delighted as usual at her quick wit even at his own expense.

Within minutes she'd pulled into the driveway of an attractive little ranch house. "I'll just be a minute,'' she said.

"Whoa, I want the full tour,'' he exclaimed, stepping out of the car. "Nice,'' he commented as they walked to the front porch. He wasn't sure if he was speaking about the house or the shapely legs visible beneath her skirt. "Have you been here long?''

"Just a little over a year,'' she replied as she unlocked the front door. "I got a good deal because the person who owned it before me got transferred back to the States.'' She opened the door and gestured him inside.

He stepped into the living room and looked around with interest. The overstuffed sofa was sand-colored, with throw pillows in all the earth tones of Montebello. A medley of plants indigenous to the region grew in clay pots of various shapes and styles.

It was as if she'd brought pieces of the outside in, complete with accents of bright blue—the color of the Montebello sky. The entire effect was one of warmth and invitation.

"Very nice," he said, and watched her cheeks stain pink with pleasure.

"Thanks. I'll be right back, I've just got to grab the log from my office." She disappeared down the hallway.

Kyle wandered the room, taking in the whimsical knickknacks and the multitude of scented candles set in groups of three and four all around the room.

She not only lived here, she'd nested here, feathering her space with creature comforts and pleasures. For a long moment Kyle thought of how nice it would be to come home every night to a place like this, to a woman like Joanna.

Frowning, he shoved the disturbing thought aside and instead stepped into the kitchen. Here again, the room was decorated in earth tones, with splashes of yellow that appeared to light up the room. And again he felt a sense of welcome and warmth.

"Got it," she said, brandishing the logbook as she walked into the kitchen. "Shall we get to the base?"

"Aren't you going to show me the rest of your place before we go?"

He wanted to see her bedroom, the place where she slept...and dreamed. She hesitated only a moment, then gestured for him to follow her down the hall.

She opened the first door to reveal an office. The room was strictly functional and devoid of personality. A desk, neat and orderly, sat in the center of the room, a computer upon it.

The bathroom carried on the earth-tone theme and sported a seashell motif.

When she opened the door at the very end of the hallway, Kyle caught his breath. Here was the essence of Joanna. The unmade bed was an explosion of reds and pinks, and a lacy beige nightgown was thrown across the foot.

He caught a glimpse of more candles on the nightstand, along with several bottles of lotions and a stack of paperback books.

"It's kind of a mess. I didn't have time to get things in order after you called," she said, and shut the door before he'd gazed his fill. "And that's it. It's just a two-bedroom house."

He followed her back into the living room, but when she started for the front door, he lingered in the center of the room.

"Don't you want to know?" he asked.

She frowned in bewilderment. "Don't I want to know what?"

"What this place says about you—the personality traits that are exposed here."

She grinned and her dark eyes danced in obvious amusement. "Sure, let's see if your theory flies or fails." The beauty of her open, genuine smile lit sparks in the pit of his stomach.

He advanced closer to where she stood, not stopping until he was close enough to feel her body heat, close enough to see the definition of each of her long, thick eyelashes and the sudden wariness in her eyes.

He also felt the tension that gripped her and knew that he was invading her personal space by standing so close. But he wanted to invade her personal space. The desire that had been growing inside him for the past four days now seemed to fill each and every cell within him.

"First of all, your choice of colors shows an earthy side of you, a bond with nature." He reached up and touched an errant strand of her hair that had managed to escape from the barrette. How he wanted to release all of it, allow those dark, rich strands to spill over his hands.

Her eyes widened, but she didn't step back from him, did nothing to break the fragile physical contact. "Your office showed me that you take your work very seriously. You're conscientious and goal-oriented and highly efficient."

"You could have guessed all that simply by the job I hold," she said, her voice slightly breathless.

His finger moved from her hair to the side of her cheek. Her skin was warm...so invitingly warm. He thought he could hear her heart beating—or perhaps it was his own pounding loudly in his ears.

"You want to know what else I've learned about

you?'' His voice was a mere whisper as his gaze locked with hers.

She nodded slowly and her tongue slid out to quickly dampen her lips. Kyle felt his control slip more than a notch.

''The scented candles that you have everywhere tell me that you have a sensual soul.'' He rubbed a finger over her full lower lip.

Her lips parted as if of their own volition. Fire licked at his insides. ''The red-and-pink sheets and things in your bedroom, the lacy nightgown you wear to sleep, all tell me that you have a well of passion deep inside you just waiting to be tapped.''

He couldn't stand it another minute; he had to kiss her. The need was overwhelming, almost frightening in its intensity. He didn't resist, but gave into it, allowing it to consume him fully.

He wrapped her in his arms and claimed her lips with all the hunger that gnawed at his insides.

She didn't fight the kiss. Her mouth opened to welcome him, although her arms remained at her sides. Her lips were just as he remembered—wonderfully soft and filled with a sweet, evocative heat.

He'd been hungry for her for three long months, and now that she was in his arms, blood surged inside him and his body instantly responded to her curves, so close against him.

He slid his tongue into her mouth, wanting to taste all of her, and his desire soared even higher when her tongue met his, dueling in mutual exploration.

He could lose himself right here, right now with her. There was nothing he wanted more than to sweep her up in his arms and carry her into her bedroom. There was nothing he'd like more than to make love to her amid those colorful sheets, which he knew would smell of her.

The thud of the logbook falling to the floor pulled him back to reality, and the realization that he didn't want to make love to her with a workshift hanging over his head.

He didn't want to have to hurry so they could make it to the base in time. The next time he made love to her, he wanted it to be slow...with no pressure of time, nothing to think about but the pleasure of Joanna.

He released her and she stepped back, her eyes as dark as he'd ever seen them. "You shouldn't have done that," she said, then leaned down to pick up the logbook she'd dropped.

"Why not?"

She straightened, her gaze not meeting his, but rather darting around the living room behind him. "Because as you were getting clues to my personality, you should have realized that I like my life just the way it is, without complications."

"I don't want to be a complication," he replied, then grinned. "I just want to bring a little pleasure into your life."

She swept her gaze up and down the length of him, as if silently taking stock of him as a man. "It's egotistical of you to presume that I found your kiss pleasurable." She didn't wait for his response, but turned and stepped out the front door.

Kyle followed, his confidence suddenly shaken more than he cared to admit.

Joanna felt bad. And it made her mad that she felt bad. Kyle Ramsey was arrogant and cocky and far too sure of himself, and she shouldn't feel bad for having put him in his place.

Still, she couldn't help but feel a little bit sorry for what she'd said to him. He'd looked so surprised, so shocked at the idea that she might not find his kiss pleasurable. And what made her feel worst of all was the fact that her words had been such a blatant lie.

She had found his kiss more than pleasurable. The feel of his warm lips against hers had rocked her to her very core, had set off tiny explosions of intense pleasure in every single one of her nerve endings.

That kiss had sought out and found all the cold, empty places inside her, and warmed them, filled them up.

If that kiss had lasted for one more minute, he would have been able to do whatever he wanted with her and she wouldn't have had the strength or the desire to protest. She'd been completely and utterly under his sensual spell for the duration of that kiss.

"Eagle One to base." His deep, smooth voice sounded in her earphone.

"Eagle One, this is base. Go ahead."

"I'm coming in."

She looked at her watch and realized it was finally time for their shift to be over. It had been a long night. She'd grown accustomed to Kyle keeping up a teasing patter while he was in the air and she was on the ground, but not this time.

He'd radioed her only when necessary, his voice cool and professional and devoid of anything personal. And wasn't that exactly what she wanted?

Seeing that her shift replacement had put on a headset and was ready to take over, she yanked off her own earphones. She stretched her arms overhead, working out the kinks that had taken up residency from her sitting in the same chair for so long.

Outside the window, the sun was just lighting up the sky, announcing another day of dry desert heat and cloudless blue heavens. At least this dawn hadn't brought any morning sickness with it, she thought as she gathered her belongings for the drive home.

By working all night, she'd tricked her body into skipping the usual nausea. Instead, she felt the pangs of hunger gnawing at her. It had been several weeks since she'd actually looked forward to eating breakfast, but at the moment breakfast sounded wonderful.

As usual, when Kyle walked into the operation center he brought a restless energy with him. He said not a word to anyone, but went directly into the adjoining room to change out of his flight suit.

When he returned, he nodded to Joanna, letting her know he was ready to leave. Silently they left the building and got into her car.

It amazed her that he seemed to be giving her the silent treatment. She'd always heard that the male ego was fragile, but she would have never guessed that Kyle Ramsey's ego was anything close to vulnerable.

They drove for a few minutes in silence. Finally she broke the uncomfortable quiet. "You're pouting," she exclaimed.

"Excuse me?" He turned and stared at her, those gray eyes of his cool and assessing.

"You're pouting because I indicated I might not have enjoyed your kiss."

"Don't be ridiculous. I'm an adult and I certainly don't pout," he scoffed, but she thought she saw a telltale reddening of his cheeks as he directed his attention out the window.

They rode in silence once again for the next several minutes. Where always before she felt an invigorating energy rolling from him after a shift, this morning she felt an uncomfortable tension. She turned the car radio on low to fill the tense silence.

"Okay," he said, and released a deep sigh. He leaned forward and turned off the radio. "I'll admit it, maybe I am pouting just a little bit."

"I thought so," she said with a smile of satisfaction.

"What I want to know is what did I do wrong? I've never had any complaints before and if I'm slipping, it's important that I know. Was the kiss really unpleasant for you?"

She felt his gaze on her, intent and serious, and she didn't know whether to laugh or not. It was so ridiculous for him to be worried about whether or not she'd liked his kiss.

She cast him a quick glance and that was a mistake. Seeing the utter seriousness, the genuine worry in his eyes, she couldn't lie. "No. I didn't find it unpleasant,'' she finally confessed, and refocused her attention on the road, although she could still feel his gaze on her.

''If you were rating the kiss on a scale of one to ten, ten being one of the best kisses you've ever had in your life, what would you give my kiss?''

She laughed and shook her head ruefully. ''You are utterly incorrigible. Why is it so important what I thought of your kiss?''

''Because I'm always looking for ways to make self-improvements. If you think my kiss was only a five or a six, then maybe you'll have recommendations about how I can improve.''

She glanced at him once again, to see if he was being serious, and was unsurprised to see the teasing, amused glint in his eyes. ''You know you're a good kisser. You don't need my opinion to swell your head,'' she replied as she pulled up in front of his apartment building.

''So, it was a ten?''

''Absolutely not. At best it was an eight or a nine.'' She put her car into park and turned to gaze at him once again. ''A ten can only be achieved through marriage. When a groom kisses his bride, that's a ten. When a husband kisses his wife, that's a ten. Anything outside of marriage can only be a nine.''

''That's not true. With enough practice, I'm sure I could achieve a ten with you.''

''You won't be in Montebello long enough to get that much practice,'' she countered.

He laughed and unfastened his seat belt. ''Why

don't you come up and let me cook us some breakfast?''

She wanted to. Lord knew she desperately wanted to. She had a feeling if she agreed and went with him to his apartment, breakfast might lead to another kiss…and another kiss might lead to something else.

"I'd better get on home," she said, wondering if her regret was in her voice for him to hear. "I'm tired. It's been a long night."

"You sure? I make a mean omelette." His mouth was talking about eggs and toast, but those gorgeous, seductive eyes of his were speaking of something else altogether.

"I'm positive." She put her car into gear to let him know she wasn't going to change her mind. Or maybe it was to make sure she didn't change her mind.

"Then I guess I'll see you Thursday." He opened his car door and stepped out.

"That's right. We have tomorrow and tomorrow night off. I'll pick you up at six on Thursday morning." Funny, the thought of not seeing him the next day was a letdown. She was quickly growing accustomed to his company. He had a wicked sense of humor, and as much as she hated to admit it, she enjoyed being around him.

A moment later, as she pulled away from the curb, she fought the impulse to turn the car around and go back to his apartment.

The kiss they'd shared earlier had stirred her up inside, made her remember how wonderful making love to him had been. They'd come together explosively, and Joanna had a feeling that kind of chemistry, that kind of physical compatibility, only happened once in a lifetime.

What frightened her more than anything was that while he'd been kissing her, she'd entertained the thought of going to bed with him again. What had scared her was that even knowing he was all wrong for her and there could never, ever be a future for the two of them together, she still wanted him.

Chapter 5

Joanna was curled up in bed reading a book called *Nine Months, A Guide for Pregnant Women* when the ringing of the nearby phone interrupted her.

She placed the book on the bed next to her and reached for the phone on the nightstand. "Hello?"

"Were you sleeping?" Kyle's familiar voice filled the line and instantly created a tiny ball of heat in the pit of her stomach. He had the deepest, sexiest voice.

"I was until about ten minutes ago. I've just been lying here contemplating getting up," she replied, and looked at the clock on her nightstand. Almost two in the afternoon. She'd slept for nearly six hours. "When this is all over, I'm definitely going to have my days and nights mixed up."

"I'm sure these hours are a little rough on you, since you're used to a normal daily schedule."

"I'll survive," she replied. "What's up?"

"Well, I've got a new kink to throw into today's schedule."

"What's that?" Joanna sat up and plumped the pillows behind her, then leaned back once again.

"We've been invited to the palace for dinner this evening as honored guests of King Marcus and Queen Gwendolyn."

"You are kidding." Joanna sat up once again as excitement winged through her. Dinner with the king and queen!

"No joke," he replied. "I would assume the dress is formal, and we're to be there at seven. I figure you should pick me up by six-thirty."

"Okay," Joanna replied, her mind already racing to the biggest dilemma the night would bring—what to wear. "I'll see you at six-thirty." She started to hang up, but stopped as she heard him call her name.

"Are you still in bed?" he asked.

All thoughts of appropriate dress for a dinner with the king flew out of her mind as she heard the heavy sensuality that deepened Kyle's voice. "Yes," she replied slowly. "Why?"

"I was just wondering if you were wearing that sexy little lacy nightgown I saw on the foot of your bed yesterday."

That's exactly what she was wearing, but she wasn't about to confess that fact to him. "Actually, I'm wearing a faded purple T-shirt, red fuzzy socks and I have pink foam curlers in my hair."

He laughed, the deep sexy rumble sending heat

coursing through her. "Nothing turns me on more than pink foam curlers," he replied.

"I'll see you at six-thirty," Joanna said, and hung up, a smile still curving her lips.

The smile fell away as she realized she had only about four hours to get ready to make an appearance in front of a king.

Those four hours flew by. Joanna took a long, leisurely bath, then set about trying to figure out what to wear. Her wardrobe was rather limited in that she usually spent her money on office clothing rather than fancier, classier evening wear.

As she pulled on first one dress, then another, she realized she had a second problem. Not only was she limited by the small selection of gowns, some of the more fitted styles had simply become too tight.

The baby was making itself known not only with the bouts of morning sickness she suffered, but also in more apparent physical ways. Joanna's breasts were larger, and her tummy was no longer flat, but rather displayed a small, telltale paunch.

She finally settled on a pale blue sleeveless dress with silver accents. Although the neckline was deep, the waist was an empire style that detracted from her pregnant stomach.

She used her curling iron on her hair, allowing it to fall freely around her shoulders. Adding silver earrings and a spritz of perfume, she finally left her house to drive to Kyle's apartment.

As she drove, her excitement at being an honored guest of the king and queen was tempered by thoughts of her pregnancy. Sooner or later she was going to have to make some difficult decisions.

There was no way she could continue her current work schedule at the embassy and be the kind of mother she intended to be. She didn't want her child to be raised by hired help as she had been. No way did she intend to do to her child what her father and his lifestyle had done to her.

Family. That's what the baby represented to her. At last she would have a bond, a connection—a family of her own. Family was what she'd lacked as a child, and that lack had left a hole inside her, a well of emptiness and loneliness.

She'd returned to Montebello and had taken her position at the embassy in hopes of making a family connection with her mother's family. And while she found those relatives pleasant enough, too many years had passed for her to establish any real loving bond with them.

She didn't visit her grandmama often, for in her eyes Joanna always saw sorrow for the daughter she had lost. Even though it was irrational, because Joanna's mother had died giving birth to her, Joanna felt responsible for the sadness in her grandmother's eyes.

"You will be my family," she said to the baby inside her. According to the book she'd been reading, during the fourth month of pregnancy the baby could hear her voice, and she hoped the little one could hear love in it, feel the love Joanna felt in her heart.

She had always believed that when she built her own family, it would include a husband and father for her children. But when you got lemons, you made lemonade. Kyle Ramsey was lemons, and no amount of squeezing him would transform him into the kind of rooted family man Joanna wanted—needed—in her life.

If no man entered her life on a permanent basis, then she would just learn how to be both mother and father to her child. One thing was certain—her child would always have that sense of home, security and love.

Joanna touched her stomach once again, realizing that if their current mission lasted too long, she'd have to explain her condition not only to the people at the embassy, but to Kyle as well. And what would she tell him?

She truly had no idea what she would do if and when the time came that she had to make explanations. Would he know the moment he found out she was pregnant that the baby was his?

As she pulled in front of Kyle's apartment building, she shoved away thoughts of the tiny life she carried inside her. The decisions she faced would have to be made at another time.

At the moment she needed all her focus, all her concentration, on spending an evening not only with Kyle, but in the company of the king and queen.

Kyle Ramsey in his uniform was attractive. Kyle Ramsey in jeans and a T-shirt was handsome. But Kyle Ramsey in a sharp, neatly tailored charcoal suit was absolutely debonair and downright devastating.

When he opened the door, Joanna felt her breath catch in her throat at just how devastatingly handsome he looked. The charcoal slacks and jacket matched the color of his eyes. His white shirt was crisp and clean, the top button unfastened, allowing several dark chest hairs to peek out. He looked powerfully built, yet elegant at the same time.

"Wow, you look fantastic." The first words out of his mouth were accompanied by the heat of his gaze sweeping slowly down the length of her.

Joanna felt the power of that gaze deep inside her. It was as if his fingers had acted in concert with his eyes, touching her here, there, everywhere. "Thank you," she replied. "You clean up pretty good yourself."

He flashed her a sexy grin. "Do you know how to tie a tie?" He held up a gray-and-black necktie. "I can never get them right."

She took the tie from him and set her car keys on the coffee table. "You're in luck, Lieutenant Commander. I just happen to be an expert at tying ties." She reached up and flipped his collar up, then looped the tie around his neck.

The intimacy of their positions filled her with heat. She tried to keep her gaze focused solely on the tie, wanting to get it knotted as quickly as possible so she could step away from him.

"Mmm, you smell good," he said, that smooth voice of his increasing her body temperature.

"Thanks," she said. She frowned, for her fingers seemed to be all thumbs, refusing to cooperate in the simple task of tying the tie. He smelled good, too— a clean, slightly spicy scent of cologne and male.

"It should be against the law to look as gorgeous

as you do at this moment," he murmured. She tensed as his hands moved to her shoulders. "If that neckline was just an inch lower, you definitely would be arrested."

She looked up at him worriedly. "Perhaps it's too much? Maybe I should go home and change?"

"Not on your life." His hands moved just a touch, caressing her, his fingers teasing the bare skin of her upper arms. "You look stunning and the dress is just perfect. The only thing more perfect would be if I were taking it off of you right now."

The image his words inspired caused a small flutter of anxiety—or was it anticipation?—to sweep through her. She finished the tie and stepped back, away from the heat of his body, the touch of his hands, and out of the magnetic field of his smoky eyes.

"I don't think we have time for you to take a cold shower before we go," she replied, "so you'd better just get that idea right out of your head."

For a single moment his gaze remained locked with hers. "I haven't been able to get that idea out of my head for the past five days. Ever since I saw you again that's all I've been thinking about."

Her cheeks burned as she broke the gaze and picked up her keys from the coffee table. "We'd better get going. We don't want to be late." Her voice sounded shaky, even to her own ears. Drat the man, anyway, she thought.

"You're right, we don't want to be late." He ushered her out of the apartment, his hand lingering on the small of her back while they waited for the elevator. "You can ignore me all you want, but I know the truth." He leaned down and whispered in her ear, "There's a small part of you that wants me to remove that dress, that wants me to make love to you again."

The elevator doors opened and Joanna hurried inside, a blush warming her cheeks. He was wrong. Dead wrong. It wasn't a small part of her that wanted him to make love to her again, it was a huge part.

She knew she had to decide if she could make love to Kyle Ramsey again and simply enjoy the act, without getting emotionally involved with the man.

The very last thing she wanted to do was fall in love with the father of the baby she didn't intend to tell him existed.

If Kyle had his way, he'd have said to hell with the king and queen, and swept Joanna up into his arms and carried her into his bedroom. There he would have slid that silky blue dress off her and made languid, passionate love to her until the wee hours of the morning.

But, of course, he didn't do that. Instead he sat in the car next to her, breathing in her intoxicating scent and remembering the satiny feel of her skin and the hot, sweet taste of her mouth.

He couldn't keep his eyes off her. She looked so lovely in the ice-blue dress that he ached inside, wanting her. Her hair, instead of being contained at the nape of her neck as it normally was, spilled in loose curls to her shoulders. Her makeup enhanced the dark mystery of her eyes and the lush fullness of her lips.

Tonight she looked much like the woman who had so captivated him that night in the bar—ultrafeminine and sexy as hell.

"Have you met King Marcus before?" he asked, trying to get his mind back on the evening to come. If he didn't get the image of her in his bed out of his head, he would be stark, raving mad before the night was over.

She nodded. "Several times, but always at official functions with hundreds of other people. I've never been to the palace before as a guest. What about you? Have you met him?"

"Not personally, although he and my father have known each other for years. In fact, King Marcus gave my father the land for the plant. Did I mention that you look utterly fantastic?"

Kyle watched dark color claim her cheeks. "More than once," she replied.

"So, I guess it would be redundant to tell you again."

"Redundancy isn't all bad." Her lips curved upward and Kyle chuckled. Not only did she make him want to rip her clothes off and make love to her, she also made him laugh. She was frighteningly delightful.

He focused his attention back out the window, where the palace had come into view. He needed to shove aside his desire for Joanna and concentrate on the business at hand.

He wondered if he might get an opportunity to

speak to King Marcus about the Noble Men, who were financing the operation.

Kyle would certainly like to learn more about the mysterious group that had brought him here for this particular mission. Where else had the power of these men been felt in the world? Who were they?

He glanced sideways at Joanna, wondering if she knew anything about them. If so, had she been sworn to secrecy, as well?

Their car was stopped at the palace gates and both of them showed identification before being allowed through.

Their IDs were checked again as they entered the palace itself, and both of them were gone over with a metal-detecting wand.

Kyle wondered if security had always been this strict, or if this was something new since the heightened tensions between Montebello and Tamir. He thought of the bombing. No wonder security had been increased since last time he'd been on the island.

Once they had been cleared, a man appeared to take them to the private quarters of the king and queen. Kyle was vaguely surprised that they were being taken to the inner sanctum of the palace, the area few citizens had ever been in.

As they walked down the wide marble hallway, Kyle placed a hand at the small of Joanna's back. Through the thin material he could feel her body heat. He could also feel the delicate column of her spine, and a wave of unexpected protectiveness swept through him suddenly.

He dropped his hand. Apparently his desire for her was manufacturing emotions he'd prefer not to entertain. What he needed was to get her into his bed, indulge himself in taking his fill of her, and get her firmly and forever out of his system.

They came to a private elevator operated by punching in a code on a keypad. "Enjoy your evening." The man who'd escorted them this far stepped out of the elevator, leaving Kyle and Joanna alone as the doors closed. The elevator took them to the top floor, where apparently the royal family made their home.

Once there, Kyle and Joanna stepped out of the elevator and were faced by another large, locked door. Kyle knocked and the door was opened by a uniformed housekeeper.

"Lieutenant Commander Ramsey and Ms. Morgan. Please come in." With a warm smile she ushered them into a small reception room. "If you will have a seat, King Marcus and Queen Gwendolyn will be with you momentarily."

Together Kyle and Joanna sat on the elegant brocade love seat. "You nervous?" he asked her, and reached for her hand, not surprised to find it cold.

"A little."

"Me, too," he admitted. She sent him a grateful smile that warmed the pit of his stomach. "I'm a simple man. Dining with kings and queens always makes me a little nervous."

"I have a feeling you are anything but a simple man, Kyle Ramsey," she replied softly, and pulled her hand from his.

Before he could question her about the comment, Marcus Sebastiani, King of Montebello, entered the room.

The king was a handsome man with olive skin, dark eyes and a headful of beautiful white hair. Tall, with broad shoulders, he looked physically fit despite being in his late sixties.

Both Joanna and Kyle stood and bowed as the king greeted them. "Welcome to our home," he said. "It is a pleasure to have you here. Please, come with me. The queen is awaiting us in the living room."

They followed the king down an elegant hallway and into a large room that was obviously the heart of their home. The furniture was luxurious, yet comfortable. Family pictures hung on the walls. It was apparent that while this was the living quarters of royalty, it was also the home of a family.

Queen Gwendolyn rose from her chair as they entered. Although Kyle had seen pictures of her, he'd never met her in person, and the first thing that struck him was her legendary aristocratic beauty and the genuine warmth of her smile.

"Welcome," she said, grasping first Joanna's hand, then Kyle's. "Dinner will be ready shortly. I hope you don't mind that we decided to have you here in our private quarters rather than downstairs in an official reception area."

"We are honored to be here," Kyle replied.

"We are the ones who are honored by your helping our country in this time of crisis," King Marcus said. "But right now we'll talk of more pleasant things."

A maid entered the room and poured drinks, then disappeared, leaving the four to chat. The conversation was light and flowed effortlessly. They spoke of an upcoming art festival and some of the queen's favorite charities.

The affection that existed between the king and queen was obvious, and Kyle found himself watching the interplay between the two with interest.

What must it be like to be married for many years, to live with a person who knew your innermost thoughts and dreams? What was it like to share the kind of implicit trust, complete familiarity and unwavering passion that existed in a successful marriage?

His parents shared the same kind of bond. They could look at one another and Kyle knew they were communicating in a language known only to them.

He shoved these thoughts aside as they were taken into a formal dining room for their meal, where they were joined by two of the king and queen's daughters, Princess Anna and Princess Julia.

Kyle studied the two women. Princess Anna was obviously the apple of her father's eye, he soon realized. Of the two, she looked most like her father.

Princess Julia had the fair complexion and blue eyes of her mother, and dark brown, shoulder-length hair. She seemed subdued throughout the meal, and Kyle remembered what he'd heard about her—that she was supposedly pregnant with Sheik Rashid Kamal's child. And Sheik Rashid Kamal was missing.

Kyle wondered what could have driven the princess into the arms of the son of her father's enemy.

The feud between the Sebastiani and Kamal families had been long standing, but Kyle didn't know exactly what had caused it or when it had first begun. He made a mental note to ask Joanna if she knew the history of the feud.

His gaze lingered on Joanna. She'd impressed him throughout the evening. Although some men might have found the queen, with her pale blond hair and elegant features, the most beautiful woman in the room, Kyle thought Joanna outshone her.

Not only was she beautiful, but she proved to be a gracious guest and seemed completely at ease no matter where the conversation strayed. She could talk about flowers and art, or politics and policy.

After the meal, the king invited Kyle into his private office, leaving the women to enjoy after-dinner drinks and woman talk in the living room.

"I'd offer you a drink, but I noticed you had none before dinner," King Marcus said.

Kyle smiled. "It's best to fly planes without a hangover."

The king nodded and gestured him into a chair. "I can't tell you how my country appreciates what you and your men are doing here. I don't know what we would have done had the Noble Men not offered their support."

Kyle drew a deep breath and leaned forward. "Your highness, what can you tell me about the Noble Men who brought me here?"

The king sat in the chair opposite Kyle's. "I'm afraid there is nothing specific I can tell you about the Noble Men. I can tell you that they are honorable men who have devoted their lives and resources to people, not governments. They are men who grew frustrated by the red tape of bureaucracy and made a conscious choice to work outside the boundaries."

"But who exactly are they?"

The king smiled and shook his head. "I'm sorry, Kyle. I can say no more. I am bound by my honor to a code of silence."

Frustration flurried through Kyle, but he knew better than to push the king on the subject. "Your daughters are lovely women," he said. "You must be very proud."

"I am," the king replied.

"I understand one of your daughters works and lives in the States."

King Marcus nodded. "Christina is in Montana and doesn't visit home often enough to suit us. We miss her dearly." He shook his head, suddenly looking older than his years. "These are sad times, Lieutenant Commander, and frightening times for my people."

He stood and walked over to a set of windows, his back to Kyle. "Each night I stare into the darkness and pray for my son's return to his country and his family. And now I find the son of a man who wants nothing but our land has apparently seduced my daughter and disappeared like a thief in the night."

He turned to face Kyle, his dark eyes blazing with suppressed anger. "And now Kamal accuses me of crimes against his son and threatens the security of my country. The entire situation is untenable."

Drawing a deep breath, he once again sat across

from Kyle, the flames in his eyes gone, replaced by a profound sadness. "That Kamal would believe me capable of harming his son when I'm reeling from the loss of my own is absolutely unforgivable."

"There has been no word about Prince Lucas?"

"No. The search of the airplane crash site continues, but still his body hasn't been found." The king stared down into his drink, and Kyle knew his thoughts were for his firstborn son. "You aren't married, are you?"

Kyle shook his head, and the king continued, "Then you can't know the pain of hearing the woman you love more than life itself crying in the night, mourning for her firstborn son. Her sobs echo deep inside my heart. Her tears scald the skin of my cheeks."

Would he ever experience that kind of love? Kyle wondered. He'd certainly never gone looking for it. He liked his lifestyle just the way it was—footloose and fancy free and bound to nobody. Still, that kind of soul connection, that intense love, surely must be wonderful.

The conversation turned to less personal things, and within an hour Kyle and Joanna were saying their goodbyes to the royal family.

"Tired?" Kyle asked as they walked from the palace to where Joanna's car was parked.

"Not really. Just rather relieved that the night is over." She flashed him a quick smile. "I didn't realize quite how stressful dining with royalty could be."

He looked at her in open admiration. "If you were

stressed, it certainly didn't show. You were a courteous, charming guest.''

"Thank you," she replied, a blush of pleasure coloring her cheeks. "I think we both managed ourselves quite well."

"At least I didn't spill anything down the front of me or use the wrong fork," Kyle said.

They got into her car, and instantly he was treated to the faint fragrance of her perfume, the familiar scent that had haunted him for months.

As she pulled away from the palace, Kyle looked at her, his eyes feasting on the swell of her breasts above the plunging neckline. She was so beautiful, and never had he seen her looking lovelier than she did at this very moment.

He recognized that he'd been on a slow simmer all night, watching Joanna in her sexy dress, listening to the melodic sound of her laughter, watching her beautiful eyes sparkle and dance.

In fact, he'd been on a slow simmer every minute of the past five days.

And tonight, if he had his way, the simmer was going to explode to a full boil.

Chapter 6

"Tell me about the history of the feud between Tamir and Montebello. Do you know when it started?" Kyle asked as they drove back to his apartment.

Joanna frowned, remembering when she'd first returned to Montebello and had studied the history of the island. "It's a tragic story. It started back in the late 1800s, when a wedding was supposed to take place between the Sebastiani and Kamal families. Sheik Mukhtar Kamal's son, Sheik Omar, was to marry King Augustus Sebastiani's daughter, Princess Delia."

"Let me guess—the wedding didn't come off," Kyle said.

Joanna nodded, trying to ignore how the pleasant scent of him in the small confines of the car seemed to seep into her every pore.

"Land and trade agreements were drawn up in anticipation of the union. Part of Montebello was designated to go to the sheik as Princess Delia's dowry, and in exchange, an important trade agreement between Montebello and Tamir was sealed. Then large deposits of copper were discovered on the land that was to be given as the dowry, and everything fell apart when Sheik Omar was mysteriously killed just a few days before the wedding was to take place."

"So what happened to Princess Delia?"

"Supposedly she was overcome with grief and killed herself. King Augustus, distraught over his daughter's death, reneged on his vow to share his land with Tamir. Sheik Mukhtar thought the king had something to do with his son's death and waged war, trying to take Montebello by force."

Kyle whistled. "A regular Romeo and Juliet kind of a story. It almost sounds like history is repeating itself. Missing sons, grief and war." He shook his head ruefully. "A sad state of affairs."

Joanna thought of Princess Julia—supposedly pregnant by the handsome sheik who was now missing. What must the princess be going through? How heavy could her heartache be? Throughout dinner, although Princess Julia had been quite gracious, Joanna had seen shadows in her eyes…the shadows of shattered dreams. And in those moments she had felt a curious affinity for the lovely, pregnant young woman who might find herself raising a child all alone.

Joanna sighed. "These two families seem to be cursed. I feel so badly for Princess Julia."

"She didn't look pregnant. What makes everyone think that she is?"

"Apparently she told somebody, then somebody told somebody else. You know how these things go…it's very difficult to have any secrets if you're part of the royal family. There are always 'inside sources' willing to tell secrets for cash."

Kyle reached over and wrapped his hand around her wrist, his fingers warm and strong. "If you tell me your secrets, I promise I will never sell you out."

Despite the cool air blowing from the air conditioner vents, a wave of warmth suffused Joanna at the touch of his hand. "I don't have any secrets," she replied, mentally crossing her fingers.

His fingers uncurled from her wrist, only to run lightly up her arm toward her shoulder. "You have the softest skin," he murmured.

"Kyle, you're making it difficult for me to concentrate on my driving," she protested rather shakily. The feel of his warm fingers sent pleasure shooting through her entire body. She wanted him to stop touching her; she wanted him to never stop touching her.…

He pulled his hand away as they entered the gates of Ramsey Enterprises. The moment she drew up to the curb in front of his apartment building, he unbuckled his seat belt, then again reached out and caressed the length of her arm. "Come up and have a cup of coffee with me," he said, his voice filled with warm invitation.

"I don't think that's a good idea," she replied, fighting the overwhelming desire she felt for him. It felt as if she'd been waging this battle forever, a battle she was ill-equipped to win.

"Why not?" he asked, his fingers massaging her shoulder with just enough pressure to feel wonderful.

She turned her head to look at him. "Because I have a feeling you're offering something much more than a mere cup of coffee." She silently cursed the trembling voice that exposed her vulnerability.

His eyes were blazing infernos of gray fire, his desire for her an almost tangible force in the air. "If I am, what's wrong with that?"

What was wrong with that? As his fingers plied her shoulder with heat and his eyes beckoned her to fall into the flames, her head worked to come up with all the reasons why she shouldn't go upstairs and fall into his bed.

She certainly didn't have to worry about getting pregnant. She'd already taken that gamble and lost. She was well over the age of consent and owed her fidelity to nobody. She didn't intend to do anything irrational and stupid, such as fall in love with Kyle Ramsey.

She knew what he was offering her was a single night of pleasure and nothing more. And that was just fine with her, because she wanted nothing more than that from him. She knew at heart that what the two of them wanted in their futures was very different, and it would be the height of foolishness for her to fall for him.

"Coffee sounds good," she replied, her heart thudding a new rhythm in her chest as she realized that what she had just agreed to had nothing what-soever to do with coffee.

One night. One more night. That's what she had just agreed to. One last night of being held in his arms, of tasting the heat of his lips, of making splendid love with him.

He dropped his hand from her shoulder and instead unfastened her seat belt. "I promise to do my best to make it the best cup of coffee you've ever enjoyed."

As she got out of the car, she waited for a red light to flicker in her brain, a warning bell to jangle discordantly, but her mind remained blissfully calm.

Kyle threw his arm around her shoulder and pulled her tight against him as they went into the apartment building.

The moment the elevator door closed to take them up to the top floor, Kyle gathered her into his arms and took full possession of her mouth.

If there had been any doubt in Joanna's mind as to what she was about to do, his kiss swept it away. In all her twenty-seven years, no man had kissed her so thoroughly, with such complete mastery.

As his mouth plied hers with heat and his tongue danced sensually with her own, his hands gripped her by the lower back and pulled her firmly against him. As her hips made contact with his, she could feel that he was already fully aroused, and this knowledge only fed the fires inside her.

The kiss continued, and with one hand at the small of her back, he ran his other hand up inside her dress, dancing lightly along the back of her upper thigh.

The intimate slide of his warm hand against the silk of her panty hose caused a shiver of sheer pleasure to whip through her.

"You have made me crazy with wanting you," he whispered as his mouth left hers and danced up the length of her throat.

She tilted her head, allowing him access to her earlobe as he slid both hands beneath her dress and caressed up her thighs to her buttocks.

"The feeling is mutual," she replied breathlessly.

At that moment the elevator doors swooshed open.

Kyle stepped back from her and took her hand in his, pulling her out of the elevator and to his apartment door. He fumbled for the keys with one hand, his other hand firmly gripping hers, as if he were afraid she might change her mind and jump back on the elevator to escape.

But he didn't have to worry. Joanna had no desire to escape. There was a feeling of inevitability about the whole situation, as if she had known from the first moment she saw him again at the embassy that eventually they would go to bed together one more time.

In the last three months, not a day had gone by that she hadn't thought of that crazy, wild night she'd spent with the handsome man she'd met in the bar. He'd made her feel beautiful, and he'd made her laugh, and as they'd made love, he'd made her feel like the most desirable woman in the whole wide world.

Their shared past consisted of a single night, but

that night had been burned forever into Joanna's mind.

There was no pretense of making coffee when they entered the apartment. He took her nowhere near the kitchen. Rather, he locked the apartment door and turned to face her. Without saying a word, he scooped her up in his strong and capable arms and carried her down the long hallway to a bedroom.

He set her on the floor near the edge of the bed. The room was lit with only the moonlight that flooded in through the window, but it was enough for her to see his hunger just before he claimed her mouth again.

As he kissed her, he shrugged out of his suit jacket and tossed it on the floor, then yanked at the tie around his neck.

When he had it loose, Joanna moved her fingers to the buttons of his shirt, wanting it off, wanting to feel the hard muscles of his chest, the spring of his chest hair beneath her fingertips. As she unbuttoned his shirt, his hands seemed to be everywhere, sweeping up and down her back, then stroking upward and lingering at the sides of her breasts.

Their breathing filled the room, rapid and shallow as their excitement increased. She succeeded in unfastening his shirt, and shoved it from his shoulders, then pressed her lips against the taut, hot skin of his chest. She flicked her tongue across one of his nipples and reveled in his sharp intake of breath.

He pulled away from her and held her at arm's length, his charcoal eyes burning with fever. "You have no idea what you do to me," he said, his voice a sexy growl. "From the moment I saw you again, I haven't been able to think of anything but making love to you."

"I feel the same way," she whispered, her senses reeling beneath the sensual assault.

"I intend to love you like you've never been loved before. I'm going to start here…" he pressed his lips to her forehead "…and I'm not going to stop until I've tasted every inch of you."

Joanna's legs threatened to buckle at the sweet promise that glistened in his eyes. Thankfully, before her knees could give way, he pulled her up against him once again. She felt his heart banging against her own, the ancient rhythm of desire coursing through them both.

She wrapped her arms around his neck and pressed herself against him as his hands moved to the top of the zipper that ran down the back of her dress.

The hiss of the fastener sounded extraordinarily loud to her ears, and she knew if she intended to call a halt to what was about to happen, now was the time to do so.

But instead of calling a halt to anything, once the zipper was down, she shrugged out of the dress and allowed it to fall to her feet, leaving her clad in a slip, her underwear and her hose.

"Tell me that you want me as much as I want you," he said, and he cupped her face with his hands. His eyes were hot coals burning into hers, beckoning her to follow him into depths of passion yet unplumbed. "Tell me," he repeated.

She told him not with words, but with action. With

her gaze still locked with his, she moved her hands to the waistband of his slacks and unfastened them, then moved the zipper down.

Before she got the zipper completely undone, he stepped back from her, removed his slacks, then picked her up and placed her in the center of the bed.

He went back to his slacks and removed his wallet. He pulled out a small foil package and placed it on the nightstand.

"You don't need to use that," she said. "It's all right. I'm protected."

She knew he'd assume she was on the pill, and although that wasn't true, it was true that she couldn't get pregnant.

Before she had time to feel guilty about the half-truth, he joined her in the bed.

His lips moved to hers, stealing her breath, and she felt as if she were drowning in a sea of pleasure. As they kissed, he caressed her, the heat of his hands seeping through the silk of her slip and the lace of her underwear.

A moan escaped her as his lips left hers and moved down her collarbone, down to her silk-clad breasts. The heat of his breath against her skin caused her nipples to harden. He tongued the turgid peaks through the silk, and Joanna wanted nothing more than to remove the last of the barriers between them.

Shoving him aside, she sat up and pulled her slip up over her head and tossed it to the floor. She reached behind her to unfasten her bra, but he stopped her, taking over the task as if he delighted in undressing her.

Within minutes the two of them were naked, no barriers at all between their bodies. He slid his nakedness against hers and she reveled in the heat of him, the muscular planes that complemented her softer frame.

He seemed to be in no hurry. He took his time stroking, caressing, touching her, bringing her to the brink of fulfillment over and over again, then retreating, leaving her gasping with need.

Beneath the mastery of his touch, Joanna lost the capability to think. She could only feel, as if her brain transformed along with the rest of her to a mass of electric tingles.

When he finally entered her, he made love not only to her body, but to her mind as well, murmuring sweet endearments that sent her spinning into a maelstrom of pleasure.

And as he took complete and utter possession of her, spiraling her higher and higher, she wondered how it was possible for somebody so wrong for her to feel so incredibly right.

Kyle had made love to his share of women throughout his thirty-one years, but he couldn't remember the sensations ever being as intense as what he felt making love to Joanna.

He also couldn't remember ever having to concentrate so hard, work so diligently in order to maintain control.

As he moved his hips and felt her heat surrounding him, he focused on holding back, wanting to bring

her pleasure before ultimately allowing his own release.

The silvery flood of moonlight lit her features with
a glow, and he stared down at her, drinking of her
beauty. Her eyelids were at half-mast, as if she
were drugged with pleasure. He felt drugged also—
drugged by the sight of her, the feel of her and the
taste of her. The pressure inside him built to mam-
moth proportions.

She was not a passive lover, but rather an active
participant. Her hips thrust upward to meet him with
each stroke, and her hands tantalized his back, her
fingernails raking lightly up and down the length of
him.

He felt her rising heat, knew she was on the verge
of meltdown and increased his pace until she was
moaning, her eyes closed as she tumbled over the
precipice. As she stiffened against him and cried out
his name, he lost the last bit of his control. He
plunged headfirst into the ultimate whirlpool of pleasure, losing himself in her as she clung to him.

For a long moment neither of them moved. Grad-
ually her heartbeat, rapid and frantic against his own,
slowed to a more normal pace, and her breathing
grew more regular, as did his.

He rolled off her and onto his side, gazing at her
features in the pale moonlight. Her hair was tousled
from their exertions, and he saw the telltale shadow
of mascara just below her eyes. He thought she
looked as beautiful as he'd ever seen her.

"That was fantastic," he said softly, then leaned
forward and kissed her lightly on the lips.

"Yes, it was," she agreed when his mouth left hers. She sat up and pushed her hair away from her face.

"So, you agree...I'm a good pilot *and* a good lover?"

She laughed, a melodic sound that warmed him. "I can't answer that. I've never flown with you before."

"When this mission is over, I'll take you up for a plane ride, then you'll know the truth—that I'm not only a great lover, but a great flyboy as well."

"And just a little bit full of yourself," she added with a teasing grin. She swung her legs over the side of the bed.

"What are you doing?" he asked, a surprising edge of panic knocking inside him.

"Going into the bathroom, then I'm going to get dressed and go home."

"Don't go." The words slid from Kyle without volition. But the moment they were verbalized, he realized how much he wanted her to stay through the night. He wanted to wake up in the morning with her in his arms. "I mean, you can go into the bathroom, but don't get dressed and go home. We don't have to be at the base until noon tomorrow, and I was looking forward to fixing you one of my killer omelettes in the morning."

For a long moment she held his gaze, and in the depths of her brown eyes he saw conflicting emotions. The fact that she wasn't sure if she wanted to stay only made him want her to more.

"You owe me a morning, Joanna," he said softly.

"You sneaked out before we could have a morning together before."

"Let me think about it," she finally said, and disappeared into the adjoining bathroom, closing the door behind her.

Kyle rolled over on his back and stared up at the ceiling, wondering why he cared whether she spent the night or not. Maybe it was because if she left now it would feel too much like she was walking out on him again.

He'd never been in the position of asking a woman to stay the night. Most of the time his women were all too eager not only to stay the night, but also to move right in. What made Joanna so different?

She came back into the bedroom, and instantly he could smell the scent of soap and saw that her face was scrubbed shiny clean. No traces of mascara remained. "Surely it would just be easier for me to go on home," she said, and bent down to reach for her underclothing.

He left the bed and took her bra from her hands. "Stay," he said, his voice a soft plea rather than a stern command. "Spend the night with me."

Her eyes sought his, and in the depths of hers he saw a deep yearning that touched off an unexpected loneliness inside him.

He reached out and dragged a finger down her cheek. "Stay with me and let me wake up with you in my arms. You robbed me of that pleasure before…please don't rob me of it now."

She hesitated a moment, her dark eyes unreadable. "Okay, let's go back to bed," she replied, her voice just husky enough to send a new wave of heat through him.

They got into bed and Kyle pulled the sheet up around them, then gathered her into his arms spoon fashion. The sheet was cool, but Joanna was wonderfully warm against him.

She smelled of the familiar scents that had stayed with him for months after he had first slept with her—the scent of spicy perfume mingling with a clean, fresh smell.

His hand lightly stroked her hair, then moved around her to caress the silky skin of her stomach. Funny, how the memory worked. He hadn't remembered her breasts being quite as full, and he also had thought her tummy was flatter.

Maybe she'd gained a few pounds over the last three months, he thought. If she had, the added little bit of weight certainly didn't detract from her beauty or the fact that her body seemed perfectly matched to his.

He closed his eyes, experiencing a peace of body and soul he'd never felt before. She sighed, a tiny little feminine sound of contentment that wound its way straight to his heart.

Within minutes, Kyle slept.

He awakened as morning burst into the bedroom, spilling dawn's light through the window. During sleep, he and Joanna had changed positions, and she was now curled around his back, warming him with her body heat.

Reluctant to get up and break the contact, he remained still, although his mind began to race and he tried to work through his feelings where Joanna was concerned.

That he was incredibly physically attracted to her was a given, and it intrigued him that she seemed to want nothing more from him. He felt no cloying need, no obsessive smothering from her. In fact, it was just the opposite.

He felt an emotional distance in her, a careful guarding of her inner self. There were barriers in her that challenged him, taunted him with their impenetrable force.

It disturbed him that he wanted to get into her head. He'd never wanted to with any woman before. Why was Joanna different?

Suddenly he needed to get away from her, distance himself if not mentally, then physically. He eased out of the bed and went into the bathroom.

Moments later, standing beneath a steamy spray of hot water in the shower, he tried again to sort through his feelings.

Certainly he wasn't worried about falling in love with her. Kyle didn't intend to fall in love with any woman ever. He'd decided long ago that the traditional role of husband or father simply wasn't for him.

He did not intend to give up his career for anyone or anything, and he refused to be the kind of father his own had been—gone for half his life through duty, and gone for the rest of it through choice. Kyle had understood the duty, but when his father had left the military and began spending long hours at his job, Kyle had not understood.

Kyle had hoped that by making love to Joanna one last time he'd be able to walk away from her without a backward glance. Her scent was still on his flesh, but already he wanted her again. And that bothered him.

Maybe it was time he distanced himself from her, he thought as he grabbed the bar of soap and began to lather himself.

At that moment, the shower door opened and she stood before him, a look of hesitancy in her eyes. "Room for two?" she asked.

Any desire he'd felt for distance vanished. He grabbed her arm and pulled her beneath the steamy water, against his soapy body.

It was nearly an hour later that they sat in the kitchen with cups of coffee. He'd tried to talk her into letting him cook her breakfast, but she'd insisted she didn't do breakfast, so he'd settled for making coffee.

He sipped his brew and gazed at her above the cup. As usual, she looked lovely. Although she didn't have on a stitch of makeup, her face had the glow of a sated woman, and it pleased him to know he had been the one to put it there.

She took a drink of her coffee, then stared down into her cup. "How long do you think this mission is going to last?" she asked.

He shrugged. "Hard to tell. I suppose it will last until King Marcus feels there is no longer a threat from Tamir or until the funds run out. Could be months...could be mere days. Why?"

"Just curious. I hope it doesn't go on for too long."

"Why? You know that when it's over you're going to miss me," he said teasingly.

"Don't flatter yourself," she said dryly. "I was just wondering."

He could tell she had something on her mind, but he had no idea what it might be. "You like your work at the embassy?" he asked.

"For now."

"What does that mean?" he asked curiously.

She frowned and once again directed her gaze into her coffee cup. "I don't know. I love my job, but eventually I'll want more in my life than a job that requires most of my time and energy."

Warning signals went off in Kyle's head. "I suppose you're talking about someday having a family?" So she wasn't so unlike all the other women he'd dated, after all.

"Sure. Someday I want to get married and have children. But you have no need for that, do you?" Her gaze held his intently.

"Nope. I've never had any interest in becoming a husband or a father, and I can't imagine anything or anyone changing my mind."

She smiled. "Maybe you don't need to create a family because you had the luxury of growing up in one." She took another sip of her coffee, a reflective expression on her face. "I spent my entire childhood alone, constantly changing locations, never being anywhere long enough to make friends. Eventually I want a real home in one place, and a family of my own.''

She set her mug down and laughed. ''Don't worry, Kyle, my feminine wiles are not directed toward you. I recognize poor long-term material when I see it.''

Poor long-term material. Although that's exactly the way he'd always thought of himself, it irritated him to hear her say it. ''It's not like I'd be terrible as a husband or father,'' he protested. ''I just choose not to take my life in that direction.''

''The only direction I'm taking my life at the moment is home,'' she replied, and scooted back from the table.

Kyle got up and walked with her to the apartment door, his thoughts in turmoil. He didn't want her to go and yet needed her to leave.

''Thanks, Kyle.'' She smiled, that full-bodied smile that lit her from within and warmed him down to his toes. ''It was a terrific cup of coffee.''

He chuckled, and was still chuckling when she disappeared into the elevator. As he turned to go back into his apartment, his laughter faded and he frowned. What in the hell was he doing with her…and more importantly, what in the hell was she doing to him?

Chapter 7

"When are you going to take me to one of Montebello's beautiful beaches?" Kyle's voice filled Joanna's ear through her phone line.

She fought her surprise at hearing from him. For the past three days, ever since the night she had spent with him, he hadn't attempted to spend any time outside work with her. Although he'd been friendly, he'd definitely been distant, merely confirming to her that he certainly wasn't cut out to be a husband or a father.

"I guess if you really want to, we could go to the beach this afternoon," she replied. She looked at the nearby clock. "We could spend a couple hours there and still have time to make our shift at six."

"That sounds great. Have you eaten lunch yet?"

Joanna sat up and set her book on the coffee table.

''No, I was just contemplating lunch when the phone rang.''

''How about you pick me up in thirty minutes or so and I'll get together a picnic lunch?''

She knew she should probably say no. There was absolutely no reason for them to seek each other out outside of their work. She'd assumed he'd come to the same conclusion in the last couple of days.

She had resigned herself that Kyle Ramsey the pilot might be in her life because of their shared mission, but Kyle Ramsey the man had decided it was smart for the two of them not to spend any additional time together.

There was no denying the chemistry between them, the enormous physical desire, but both were aware that their relationship could only be that—a series of one-night stands with no future.

''Okay, sounds good,'' she heard herself say, and cursed her weakness where he was concerned. ''I'll see you in about half an hour or so.''

She hung up the phone and remained on the sofa, castigating herself for agreeing to his plan. He'd slept with her, made passionate love to her, then for the last three days had effectively ignored her.

She should be annoyed with him. She should feel used and discarded by a callous man. But she didn't. And she did so enjoy his company. He had a wonderful sense of humor, was always filled with an energy that was exhilarating, and she even found his touch of arrogance oddly charming.

Their discussion over coffee the morning after she'd stayed the night only confirmed what she had known, that Kyle Ramsey would never be—could never be—anything in her life or the life of the baby she carried.

Her biggest worry right now was how she was going to explain her pregnancy if this mission lasted months…and how she was going to wear a bathing suit without her telltale tummy exposing her secret.

It took her fifteen minutes to finally decide to wear her bathing suit with a large tank-top T-shirt over it. She could still get some sun on her arms and legs, but wouldn't expose the taut material of her suit across her burgeoning belly.

Dressed and ready to go, she went back into the living room and closed the book on pregnancy she'd been reading. She'd been reading the chapter on the fourth month of pregnancy when the phone had rung.

Joanna wanted to make sure she did everything absolutely right to ensure her own health and the health of her baby. The fact that her own mother had died while giving birth to her was never far from Joanna's mind.

While she didn't fear death herself, she feared what would happen to her baby if something did go tragically wrong. But her doctor had assured her she was a textbook case of a perfectly normal pregnancy. She and the baby seemed to be in excellent health, and he insisted she needn't worry.

Kyle was ready when she arrived at his place. He met her at his door with a huge picnic basket in one hand and two thick, fluffy beach towels, a small beach umbrella and a blanket in the other.

He handed her the beach towels and grinned boyishly. "I'm really looking forward to this. It's been a long time since I've had the opportunity to swim and enjoy a beautiful beach."

Joanna nodded, trying to ignore how handsome he looked in a pair of maroon-and-navy bathing trunks and a maroon T-shirt. He had the kind of lean, but muscular legs that looked terrific in a pair of shorts.

Within minutes the picnic basket and other items were loaded into her back seat and the two of them were on their way. "Are the beaches usually crowded?" he asked. "I hate having to fight people for a little bit of water space."

"The public beaches are always pretty packed, but I'm taking you to a private beach that a friend of mine owns."

"A private beach? Hmm, maybe we can do a little skinny-dipping," he teased.

"Not in this lifetime," she exclaimed firmly. Being naked with Kyle under cover of dark was crazy, being naked with him in the brilliant sunshine or any other time was utter madness. "Besides, there will probably be other people there, just not too many."

"I'm really looking forward to a dip in the Mediterranean. I love to swim. What about you?"

"Swimming is all right, although today I just plan to sit on the beach and soak up a little sun."

As they left the city, Kyle sat up taller in the seat and stared out the window with interest. "This is a beautiful island," he said. "And so filled with contrasts. On the one hand you've got sandy beaches and the heat of the desert, and yet there are also gorgeous mountains and green valleys."

"Yes, it is beautiful," she agreed, relaxing with each moment that passed. At least he wasn't being openly flirtatious and creating the crazy kind of heat inside her that he seemed to be able to evoke so easily. "If you could live anywhere in the world, where would you choose?"

"Hmm, that's a tough one. I know it would be someplace in the United States," he replied thoughtfully. "I've been to enough foreign countries to know the good old U.S.A. is where my heart is." He shrugged. "The good thing about my work is that just about the time I start to get bored with my surroundings, I'm sent someplace else. What about you?"

"I'd probably choose to go back to the States…maybe someplace in the Midwest. My father was stationed at Fort Leavenworth for two years, the longest we ever stayed at one base. Outside the post, Leavenworth was a nice small town filled with friendly people. I'd choose someplace like that."

"So, you're just a small-town girl at heart," he said, his voice teasing.

"I don't know about that. All I know is I have definite ideas about what I want out of life, and eventually I intend to achieve all my dreams."

"I make it easy on myself. I have no dreams."

Joanna looked at him in surprise, finding his words sad. "No dreams for yourself…for your future?"

He shook his head. "I live each day to the fullest and that's enough for me."

She turned down a road that led past several attractive homes. "The beach I'm taking you to is for the homes here. It's a small beach but absolutely breathtaking.''

''Who is the friend that allows you to use the beach?'' he asked.

''Just somebody who works at the embassy with me. Like me, he works long hours and has little time to enjoy the luxury of the beach,'' Joanna explained.

''Is this somebody you've dated?'' Although his tone was light and easy, Joanna thought she heard just a hint of tension. Jealousy? Surely not. Kyle wasn't the kind of possessive man to have ever experienced a twinge of jealousy.

She laughed easily. ''I'm not sure the men I work with at the embassy even recognize that I'm female,'' she replied.

''Then they must be not only blind, but fools as well.'' For just a moment her gaze met his, and in his she saw the familiar fires of banked desire.

At that moment the beach came into sight, and she breathed a sigh of relief as he directed his gaze out the window. ''Wow,'' he said, exactly what Joanna always thought when she got to this place on the island.

The beach itself was relatively small compared to the public beaches Montebello boasted. But this beach was a small peninsula with fine-grained sand the color of pale gold, surrounded on three sides by the bright turquoise Mediterranean.

It didn't take them long to unload their things from the car. Kyle spread out the beach blanket, then stabbed the opened umbrella deep into the sand to provide partial shade. The picnic basket went into the shade, and Joanna sat on the other side, with the bright sunshine pouring down on her.

"This is great," he said when they were all set up. They had the beach to themselves except for a couple with two children farther down the beach.

"Are you sure you don't want to go in?" he asked, and pulled his T-shirt over his head, exposing his gorgeous, firmly muscled chest.

"Positive." She closed her eyes and raised her face to the warmth of the sun. "You go ahead, I'll just relax here."

She didn't move again until she heard the sound of his footsteps walking away from her. Only then did she open her eyes to watch him as he approached the water.

She drank in the sight of him—the impossible width of his shoulders, the slender hips and lean, but muscular legs. The man was a walking advertisement for sex, and no woman could look at him and not think about what it might be like to make love with him.

Devastating. She knew making love to Kyle Ramsey was devastatingly wonderful. The only thing that would be more wonderful would be being loved by Kyle Ramsey.

She frowned, distressed by the very thought. There was no way she was going to fall in love with Kyle Ramsey and allow her heart to get hurt.

She was a modern, strong woman who was certainly in charge of her emotions enough to take the physical pleasure that she wanted without getting emotionally involved.

As she watched, Kyle dove into the waves. He resurfaced a moment later in the distance. He raised a hand and waved at her. She waved back, then focused her attention on the family down the beach.

She watched as the man lifted a little boy onto his shoulders and ran toward the water's edge. Even from this distance, she could hear the excited squeals of the child. "Daddy...go in the water! Go, Daddy!" The father complied with his son's wishes, stepping into the waves as his little boy shrieked in delight.

Daddy.

The word echoed inside Joanna.

Daddy.

From the moment she had learned of her pregnancy, she had denied to herself the importance of a father in a child's life. She'd told herself that she could be—would be—enough.

After all, she'd had a father, and that hadn't stopped her from feeling displaced, unloved and lonely. But could she be enough? Or would her baby grow up with an empty hole inside, a hole where a father's love and companionship should be?

No dreams. She thought of what Kyle had told her. She couldn't imagine not having dreams. What had happened to Kyle? Who had stolen his dreams from him? And would she want a man who had no dreams to parent her child?

She squeezed her eyes tightly closed and forced thoughts of him out of her head. He didn't want to be a father. A reluctant parent certainly couldn't give a child what it needed. Why should she care that

Kyle Ramsey didn't have dreams? He was nothing to her but a temporary good time.

And just because she wasn't going to be with Kyle didn't mean her child would grow up fatherless. Eventually, she might marry, and her child would have a loving, caring stepfather.

"But it's not the same," a little voice whispered in her head. And there were absolutely no guarantees Joanna would ever marry.

She told the little voice to shut up, and willed all thoughts of fatherhood, babies and Kyle out of her mind.

Kyle stayed in the water for nearly an hour, enjoying the physical exertion of swimming against the waves, and the warmth of the water and sun.

Finally, exhausted, he left the water and raced toward the blanket where Joanna was sound asleep. He grabbed one of the towels and dried off his face and hair, his gaze locked on the sleeping beauty before him.

Clad in a bright yellow tank top and sprawled across the royal blue beach blanket, she looked like a splash of sunshine fallen to earth.

She looked vulnerable in sleep, her mouth opened slightly, as if awaiting a lover's kiss. Her long, lush lashes fluttered as her eyes seemed to move beneath the lids, letting him know she was probably dreaming.

Was she dreaming of him? Of the two of them together between his crisp sheets? Heaven knew he'd thought of little else for the past three days.

He'd tried to stay away from her, had consciously kept their relationship professional since the night she'd stayed with him. He certainly didn't want to give her the wrong idea, make her think that somehow he was available for a forever kind of relationship.

But in the past few days he'd missed her smile…and the way she made him laugh. He'd missed flirting with her and watching her cheeks turn pink. And he'd missed holding her in his arms.

Finally, that morning, he'd awakened and wondered why he was denying himself the pleasure of seeing her. There was no reason on earth why the two of them couldn't enjoy each other's company for the duration of the mission, then say their final goodbyes to one another.

They were both adults, and he'd made it clear to her that he wasn't interested in any long-term relationship. The fact that she'd agreed to come here with him today told him that she knew and accepted the limitations.

He sank down on the blanket next to her, careful not to disturb her slumber. His attention was drawn to the family who shared the beach with them.

The two adults were building a sand castle with the children. The children's laughter rode on the light breeze to his ears, the symphonic melody of childhood happiness.

Kyle frowned and swung his attention back to Joanna, who stirred next to him, then opened her eyes. She sat up and raked a hand self-consciously through her hair. "Sorry…I guess I fell asleep."

"That's all right. Don't apologize," he replied easily.

"Did you have a nice swim?"

He nodded. "The water felt great. Are you hungry?"

"A little."

He reached out and pulled the picnic basket toward him. "I'm starving," he replied. "I worked up an appetite swimming." He opened the basket and began removing items. "We've got ham-and-cheese sandwiches, fruit, chips, and for dessert, chocolate chip cookies."

"Humm, sounds wonderful."

Her gaze was warm on him as he handed her a napkin. He wanted to tell her to stop looking at him that way, that if she continued to gaze at him with her large dewy eyes he wouldn't be responsible for his actions.

"I've got soda, canned fruit juice or bottled water," he said as he pulled the last of the food out of the basket.

"Bottled water is fine for me," she replied.

They ate in a companionable silence. Kyle appreciated the fact that Joanna didn't require him to entertain her or indulge in idle chitchat while they enjoyed the meal.

As they cleaned up after eating and packed things back in the picnic basket, their attention was drawn down the beach again, to where the family was playing catch with a large, multicolored beach ball.

"Looks like they're having fun," Joanna said, a touch of wistful envy in her voice.

Kyle thought of what little she'd told him about her childhood and his heart softened. "It must have been really hard not to have a mother," he said quietly.

"It was," she admitted, her eyes dark and somber. "Even now there are times I desperately wish she was around for me to talk to, that she could give me advice when I need it."

"You need advice? I'd be happy to share my mother. She's just full of advice, which I rarely listen to." There, that was better; the shadows in Joanna's eyes lifted and she laughed.

"Did you have a happy childhood?" she asked.

The question caught him off guard and he frowned thoughtfully. Had he had a happy childhood? On the surface, he'd always believed it had been a happy one, but watching the family play on the beach had evoked in him a tiny aching hole of emptiness.

"It was okay," he finally replied. "Although I have very few memories of my father being around."

"He was gone a lot?"

"He was gone for most of my childhood. Of course, what he was doing was extremely important. He was serving our country." Kyle heard the pride in his own voice, a pride for the man his father had been, and not for the man his father had become.

"But you missed him."

"Sure, but I understood why he was gone." Kyle's chest tightened, the way it always did when he thought of his father.

"It must have been hard on him, too."

Kyle looked at her in surprise. "What do you mean?"

She shrugged. "He lost out on all those years of watching the important, special moments of his children's lives."

"Yeah, well, it didn't seem to bother him too much." Kyle heard the bitterness in his voice and consciously willed it away. "Then he quit flying and began to build his empire, so he was still gone a lot."

She was silent for a long moment, and Kyle drew a deep breath, trying to rid himself of the familiar band that squeezed his chest.

"I'll bet you and your brothers are close," she finally said.

He smiled, grateful for the change of topic. "We fought like cats and dogs when we were kids, but we were and are thick as thieves."

She pulled her knees up to her chest and wrapped her arms around them. "Tell me about them," she said, and in her eyes he saw a hunger that was both appealing and just a little bit frightening in its intensity.

He stretched out on his side and propped himself up on an elbow. She did the same, so they were facing each other.

"Jake is rather serious and quiet. He is a perfect choice to take over Ramsey Enterprises, and seems to enjoy the position of CEO."

As Kyle spoke of his brothers, he relaxed once again. "And Tyler has no idea what he wants to do with his life. Right now he's working for my father, but that's just because he hasn't decided yet what he wants to be when he grows up." He grinned. "Tyler was the one who always got us in trouble when we were kids."

"Really? How so?"

"He'd come up with wild schemes and talk me and Jake into participating, and the end result was almost always a week of grounding for all of us."

She laughed. "I'll bet the three of you were a real handful."

"We were. I'm surprised my mother didn't give us all away."

Joanna's smile lingered on her gorgeous lips and her eyes sparkled brightly. "I wanted a brother or sister so much, I made one up," she said.

"Really? You mean like an imaginary friend?" Kyle wondered if she had any idea how beautiful she looked with the sunlight bringing out the highlights in her hair and emphasizing the rich darkness of her eyes.

"Her name was Cissy. I was ten when I decided I needed a sister. We had to set a place for her at the table and buckle her into the seat belt whenever we drove anywhere. She slept in bed next to me and we shared all my toys."

"How long was she with you?"

"For about six months...until my housekeeper killed her."

Kyle looked at Joanna in shock. "What?"

"The housekeeper who was taking care of me at that time was a mean, hateful woman." Joanna's eyes glittered darkly. "She hated Cissy, and one morning when I woke up she told me she'd accidentally run over Cissy in the car.''

"That's horrible," Kyle exclaimed, appalled that an adult would do such a thing to a child.

"It was," she agreed, then laughed, although her laughter held little humor. "It's funny, Cissy was a creation of my mind, and yet I truly believed that she'd been tragically killed by that witch. I held a little funeral in the backyard, buried the blanket I thought Cissy always used to cover up with at night, and mourned for weeks."

Kyle reached out and touched Joanna's cheek. "I wish I would have been there for you. My brother Jake could have acted the role of minister and somberly said a few words to send Cissy off into the afterlife. Tyler would have done some crazy hocus-pocus and brought her back to life."

Joanna laughed. "And what would your role have been in the tragedy?"

He leaned closer to her, so close he could feel the warmth of her breath on his face. "My role would have been to comfort the bereaved."

He placed his lips on hers and kissed her gently, sweetly, surprised to discover that he was mourning for the lonely little girl who'd had her heart broken from adult cruelty.

She was sweetly compliant to the kiss, and despite his determination to the contrary, desire reared up inside him. He tamped it down, aware that this was not the place or time for any kind of romantic clinch.

Breaking the kiss, he smiled at her regretfully. "I'd love to show you how truly good I am at consoling, but I'm afraid it's not appropriate with young children nearby.''

"That's good," she replied. "Because the beach has never been included in any of my fantasies. Sand is not very comfortable."

"So, tell me, Ms. Morgan, what are some of your fantasies?" He raised his brows in his best imitation of a leer.

She grinned. "Sorry, Mr. Ramsey, I share my fantasies only with a very select, very special few."

Although he had just been teasing, her reply also lit the fire of his curiosity, and her reticence in confiding her fantasies to him bothered him. "What's the matter, don't you trust me?" he asked.

The sparkle in her eyes dimmed somewhat and she gazed at him somberly. "Why on earth would I trust you? I know you're spending time with me right now, but you will eventually move on to the next woman who captures your fancy. That's what you military men do."

She sat up and smiled at him. "You just don't tell your fantasies and secrets to a short-term-relationship kind of man."

He had the craziest impulse to protest that he wasn't a short-term relationship, to take her in his arms and tell her he intended to be around forever and no other woman would ever capture his fancy. It was crazy, it was insane. He'd obviously fried his brain by allowing the hot sun to beat on his head for too long.

"I'm going to take one last swim, then we prob-

ably should pack it up and get changed for work,"
he said as he rose from the blanket.

She nodded, and Kyle raced toward the sea and
threw himself into the water. He stroked out some
distance from shore and tried to sort out the warring
emotions that raged inside him.

She was the perfect woman for him, one who obviously knew the score, knew she would only be a
temporary diversion in his life. She wasn't trying to
change his mind, wasn't pressuring him for any sort
of commitment and didn't seem disturbed that for
three long days he'd been distant and had not sought
her company outside of work.

So why did he care what kind of fantasies she
entertained? Why did he want to somehow heal the
wounds left by a callous housekeeper who had killed
her imaginary sister?

Okay, Joanna got to me with the sister story, he
conceded to himself. The story had sent a shaft of
compassion through him, a protective urge to defend
and comfort her.

And there was no denying the incredible physical
desire he felt for her—a desire that had once again
grown, since the last time they had made love.

She was just confusing him because she was so
unlike any other woman he had ever dated. She
didn't seem to want anything more from him than
what he was offering, and that was definitely different from his experiences in the past.

Feeling as if he was once again in control, he
swam back toward shore, where he could see her
gathering up their items to leave.

As he watched her from a distance, he again felt a jolt of need…of feverish desire. Her long legs were tanned and shapely, and she moved with a fluid grace. The bright yellow of her T-shirt was like a beacon, calling attention to the rich tones of her skin and the flashing darkness of her eyes.

Eventually he would get his fill of her, sate this maddening hunger for her. Eventually he would be finished with her and ready to move on.

But apparently not yet.

He left the water and ran toward where she stood waiting for him, a towel in hand. She laughed as he shook his head, sending droplets of water flying. "You look like a dog after a bath," she said, and scampered backward to escape the spray.

"Come back here with my towel," he exclaimed.

Her eyes twinkled mischievously. "Come and get it."

She took off running across the sand, and with a laugh, Kyle took off after her.

She was surprisingly fleet of foot as she raced away, her girlish giggles filling the air. When he finally caught her and wrapped her in his arms, the last thing he wanted from her was the towel.

Instead, he kissed her with the hunger that stirred inside him, and she returned his kiss with a responding hunger. When he finally broke the kiss, all laughter was gone from her eyes, from her lips.

"I don't know why, but I can't seem to get enough of you," he murmured softly.

"I feel the same way about you," she replied after a moment of hesitation.

"What are we going to do about it?"

A slow smile slid across her lips. "Take long cold showers?"

He laughed and hugged her closer. "That's not exactly what I had in mind."

Her dark eyes glittered. "Then what, exactly, did you have in mind?" she asked.

"Let's go back to your place and I'll show you."

Her eyes darkened to impossible depths and for a moment he thought he saw a flicker of warring emotions. "What are we waiting for?" she said, her voice husky.

If Kyle could have, he would have instantly transported them from the beach to her bedroom. The best he could do was break all speed records for loading the car and buckling himself in. It was amazing how fast he could move when he knew the prize was making love to Joanna.

Chapter 8

Joanna wondered if one of the symptoms of pregnancy was a lack of good judgment. Certainly she seemed to be displaying a lot of that particular characteristic where Kyle was concerned.

As she lay beneath her sheets, waiting for him to get out of the shower and join her, she wondered why he had the ability to make her want him despite all the reasons why she shouldn't.

She absolutely refused to consider that she might care about him more than just a little bit. She knew it was positively counterproductive to all of her dreams for herself and her future to fall even just a little bit in love with Kyle.

So what was she doing here, eagerly awaiting him? Why was her heart pounding with sweet anticipation? Why did she feel so incredibly alive at this moment as she waited for them to make love?

She was merely doing what men did all the time—taking her pleasure with no emotional ties or entanglements, she told herself. She didn't have to love Kyle in order to love making love to him.

She had to admit there was a magic between them when they were in bed together, and the magic was not only intoxicating, it was positively addicting.

There had not been a lot of men in Joanna's life, but of the few she'd been with, none had ever made her feel like Kyle did. He made her feel so beautiful, so desirable, and just a little bit vulnerable and shaky inside.

She was shaky now, her nerve endings tingling and her tummy jumpy. Excitement, anticipation and a tiny bit of knowledge that she was playing a fool's game all coursed through her.

Somehow she knew she shouldn't be here, snuggled in her floral sheets awaiting a man who'd become her temporary lover but would never be anything else in her life.

And then he was there…standing in the doorway of her bedroom, still damp from his shower and gloriously naked, his gray eyes glowing with flames that burned her to her very soul.

"I was looking forward to scrubbing your back, but you got out of the shower too quickly," he said as he approached the bed.

"I don't need you to scrub my back," she replied, captivated by the overwhelming masculinity of him, the clean male scent of him.

She raised the sheet to welcome him and he got

An Important Message from the Editors

Dear Reader,

Because you've chosen to read one of our fine romance novels, we'd like to say "thank you!" And, as a special way to thank you, we've selected two more of the books you love so well, plus an exciting Mystery Gift, to send you absolutely FREE!

Please enjoy them with our compliments...

Pam Powers

P.S. And because we value our customers, we've attached something extra inside...

Peel off seal and place inside...

EDITOR'S
FREE GIFT
SEAL
THANK YOU

Silhouette®
Where love comes alive™

e your Editor's
E GIFT
k You"

ver. Place it in space
atically entitles you to
fabulous mystery gift.

get 2 brand-new Silhouette
hese books have a cover
and $5.25 each in Canada,
solutely free.

r no obligation to buy
-ZERO—for your first
e to make any minimum
en one!

ers enjoy receiving their
uette Reader Service™. They
he delivery...they like getting
nt prices BEFORE they're
love their *Heart to Heart*
g author news, horoscopes,
ch more!

our free books you'll
But the choice is yours—
e at all! So why not take
ho risk of any kind. You'll

REE BOOKMARK. And
your Editor's Free Gift Offer,
BSOLUTELY FREE!

EE MYSTERY GIFT

RY GIFT
FREE

OM
SILHOUETTE

With our compliments
The Editors

The Editor's " Thank You" Free Gifts Include:
- Two BRAND-NEW romance novels!
- An exciting mystery gift!

PLACE FREE GIFT SEAL HERE

YES! I have placed my Editor's "Thank You" seal in the space provided above. Please send me 2 free books and a fabulous mystery gift. I understand I am under no obligation to purchase any books, as explained on the back and on the opposite page.

345 SDL DC3K

245 SDL DC3F
(S-IM-OS-08/01)

NAME   (PLEASE PRINT CLEARLY)

ADDRESS

APT.#   CITY

STATE/PROV.   ZIP/POSTAL CODE

Thank You!

DETACH AND MAIL CARD TODAY!

The Silhouette Reader Service™ — Here's how it works:

in beside her. His body slid against hers and sent luscious shivers of expectancy through her.

"Then what exactly do you need me for?" he asked as his mouth found the overly sensitive skin in the hollow of her throat.

"I need you to kiss me just like you're doing," she replied breathlessly, her heart racing in an unsteady rhythm as his lips moved down to her collarbone.

"What else?" he murmured, his lips nipping and teasing as they captured the tip of one of her breasts.

Words refused to form as every nerve ending in her body caught fire. A moan was her only response, but it seemed to be the one he was looking for.

He raised his head and took her mouth with his, burning her from the inside out with his flaming heat. His tongue battled with hers, dipping and sliding and deepening their kiss into complete intimacy.

There was no need for long, languid foreplay. From the moment his bare skin had touched hers, she'd been ready for him, and she knew he'd been ready for her, as well.

She reached down and wrapped her fingers around him, heard his responding moan of pleasure. She stroked him, loving the feel of his maleness and how her touch seemed to drive him just a little bit crazy.

He pulled her hand away and, with his mouth still in possession of hers, he entered her, his hands fiercely pulling her hips against his. She cried out, on the verge of fragmenting before he even began to move again.

"Joanna...sweet Joanna," he said as he moved deep within her. "I love making love to you."

He held her gaze and she saw not only his intense hunger, but a tenderness, a softness that sent a wave of heat not just through her body, but directly to her heart.

Joanna closed her eyes, not wanting any invasion into her heart, needing to keep a piece of herself separate from him. But, all too quickly, it was impossible to separate. As their bodies melded together, she felt the connection of spirits...of souls.

Their lovemaking was frenzied and filled with hunger, as if in the time they had been apart they had developed an insatiable appetite that was just now being satisfied for the first time in their lives.

Joanna's eyes burned with tears as she was filled with emotions and sensations too overwhelming to understand. She held Kyle tight, dragging her hands up and down his broad back, reveling in the feel of him, the touch of him, the very essence of him...

The tears spilled down the sides of her face as the tension inside her built to shattering proportions. And then she was shattering...exploding and flying toward the stars...and Kyle was there, crying her name as he shuddered against her.

Time stood still as they slowly wound their way back to earth. They clung together for long minutes afterward, neither speaking, but reluctant to break their fragile connection.

Soft light filtered in the window, the golden light of approaching dusk. It painted the surrounding room—and him—in warm tones.

He smiled down at her and, with a finger, lightly pushed a strand of her hair from her face. "Tears?" he asked, a frown instantly displacing his smile.

She laughed self-consciously, embarrassed by the depth of emotion their act had stirred in her. "Not sad tears. Everything was just so…so intense."

"It always is with us," he said as his thumb stroked over her cheek. "There's something powerful between us. It's like our bodies need each other."

She noticed he used the word *bodies,* as if to keep emotions separate. He'd made it purely physical, but for just a moment as they'd been making love, what Joanna had felt had transcended the physical.

"And as nice as this is, we really need to get dressed and get to the base." She heard the reluctance in his voice and felt the same emotion echoing in her heart.

She would have loved to remain just like this— held in his arms forever. She gently shoved at him and sat up, pushing aside this disturbing thought. "You take the bathroom in the hallway and I'll take this one," she said.

She left the bed and padded into the adjoining bathroom, closing the door behind her. "What are you doing, Joanna?" She stared at her reflection in the mirror.

Her dark eyes sparkled brightly, her cheeks were flushed and her lips were slightly swollen from his kisses. She looked like a woman who had just been thoroughly made love to…but it wasn't about love.

Sex. That's all it was and all it would ever be. She had to remember that fact. What she and Kyle shared was an intense physical hunger for one another—nothing more and nothing less.

She stepped into the shower for a quick wash, and scrubbed her skin until all traces of him were gone from her. Now, if she could just take out her brain and wash it until all thoughts of him were gone from her head…

When she'd been beneath him, she'd felt not only his body taking possession of hers, but also a tenuous emotional bond. And she'd realized he would never, ever really be out of her head…or her heart.

They would forever be bound together by the child she carried inside her. Even if he never knew of the child's existence, she would look at her child and remember Kyle.

She might have a little boy with his thick dark hair and slate-gray eyes, or a little girl with his beautiful smile. She knew she would look at her child and always remember the man who had made love to her with such passion.

Yes, Kyle would be a part of her life long after this mission was over and he walked away from her.

She finished her shower and dressed quickly, aware that the clock was ticking and they had to be at the base and Kyle up in the air within thirty minutes.

"Kyle?" she called as she stepped out of the bathroom. She noticed that he had remade the bed, leaving no visible hint of their afternoon delight. But she knew the dizzying scent of his cologne would linger in her sheets until the next time she washed them.

"Kyle?" She called again when he didn't answer

her. She left the bedroom and walked down the hall-way.

When she stepped into the living room, she saw him. He stood with his back to her, as still as a statue and clad in the clean clothes that they had picked up at his place before coming back here.

"We'd better get going," she said, and grabbed her logbook from the coffee table. "I'm sure nobody will be happy with us if we're late."

He turned slowly toward her, a strange expression on his face. It was then that she noticed what he held in his hand—the book she'd been reading whenever she got the time. The book about pregnancy.

Her heart crashed to the pit of her stomach and she felt her face blanch of color as she saw a stunned realization in his eyes.

"You're pregnant." The words fell flat—not a question, but rather a statement of fact.

She considered lying, her mind racing, searching for possible, logical reasons why she would have such a book. But the utter knowledge that shone from his eyes, and the realization that her condition was only going to get more and more difficult to hide, made her hesitate to tell any kind of lie.

And in the moment of hesitation, she realized one more fact to consider: she'd never been very good at lying, anyway. "Yes." The single word hissed out of her as if under enormous pressure.

His eyes flared wide, then narrowed, and his lips compressed thinly as he continued to stare at her. Heat from his gaze seared her, but it wasn't the heat of desire or want. Rather it was the flame of simmering anger.

Joanna's mouth was achingly dry and she was suddenly icy cold with anxiety. It wasn't supposed to happen like this, her mind screamed. He wasn't supposed to find out until she was ready with a reasonable story that would assure him that he had nothing to do with her present condition.

"When were you going to tell me?" he asked, snapping the words curtly.

She feigned surprise and attempted a bluff. "Why on earth would I tell you?"

Again his hard, gray eyes narrowed. He tossed the book on the sofa and approached her with slow, deliberate footsteps. She stiffened and took a step backward, unsure what to expect.

He stopped when he was mere inches from her, and his gaze pinned her like a helpless butterfly on a display board.

"Don't play head games with me, Joanna." He took her by the shoulders, his fingers exerting just enough pressure to let her know he was extremely angry.

"It happened that first night we were together, didn't it? When we made love that night, we made a baby. I know all the signs. I know you have to be at least three months pregnant. It's mine, isn't it? Tell me. You are carrying my baby."

She desperately wanted to escape. The moment she'd seen him again at the embassy, this was the scene she had dreaded, had wanted to avoid at any cost. But now that she was in the middle of it, her mind raced desperately.

If she told him the truth, it would only complicate everything. He'd made it more than clear to her that he didn't want a wife, a family. There was really no point in him knowing the truth.

"I was already a week or two pregnant when I met you that night in the bar," she said, unable to hold his gaze as the lie slid from her mouth.

He dropped his hands from her shoulders and reeled back a step. He worried a hand through his hair and his gaze held hers. "I don't believe you." His voice was far too calm and controlled for her comfort.

"Believe what you want," she replied with a forced flippancy.

"Then whose baby is it?"

Again Joanna's mind worked double time. "Somebody I dated from the embassy. We broke up a couple of days before I met you." Again she couldn't quite look at him, hated the deceit she was spinning with each and every word. "That's why I was in the bar that night. I was feeling blue about the breakup and decided to kick up my heels a little."

"What's his name?"

"Na-name?" Joanna looked at Kyle blankly.

"The name of the man you were dating. The name of the father of your baby."

"What difference does it make?"

"I want to know his name."

She looked around the room frantically, her mind

racing. Her gaze fell on a paperback mystery book she'd been reading. The author's name was Gary Warren. She looked back at Kyle.

"Gary. His name is Gary, and anything else about him is really none of your business," she exclaimed with a touch of bravado.

He said nothing, and she forced herself to hold his gaze. His features were set in stone, his eyes cold slabs of granite. "We need to get to the base," he said, and turned toward the front door.

Joanna followed, somehow knowing this conversation wasn't over and the worst was yet to come.

They rode to the base in silence—an oppressive silence that sent dread shooting through her. Kyle stared straight out the front window, a thick tension rolling from him.

She wanted to say something, but didn't know what to say, was afraid that anything she might say at this very moment would only serve to make him angrier. He didn't believe her story. She knew he hadn't believed her lies.

Her body still retained the heat of his caresses. Her lips still burned from the searing kisses they had shared. But her heart was heavy. This was the end of their relationship. It was over…and she hadn't been prepared to say goodbye.

It wasn't until she pulled her car into a parking space at the base that he turned to her, his facial features devoid of all expression. "This isn't over yet, Joanna. I don't believe you were already pregnant that night we met. And if I find out you're lying to me, I promise you there's going to be hell to pay."

He didn't wait for her reply, but jumped out of the car and headed for the building.

She shut off her engine and locked the car doors, then hurried after him, but by the time she got to their operation area, he was nowhere to be found.

"Ah, the relief team has arrived," Scott Burwell, another of the pilots who helped Joanna with ground support, exclaimed at the sight of her. "Lieutenant Commander Ramsey must be eager to get in the air. He zoomed in here, grabbed his flight suit and flew outside."

Joanna sat down next to him, put on the headset, then offered Scott a forced smile. "I'm all set, so you're free to get out of here."

Scott pulled off his headset and reared back in his chair. "Things are quiet on the home front," he said.

"We like things quiet," she replied. If only he knew how unquiet things were on her personal home front.

"Base, this is Eagle One ready for takeoff." Kyle's voice filled her ears.

"Eagle One, you're clear," she replied after checking the air traffic screen.

"I'm taking off," Scott said. "See you later."

"Okay, see you," Joanna replied, grateful to be alone. The room was silent except for the sound of the two pilots talking to one another in her headset. It would be thirty minutes before somebody joined Joanna in the operations room to aid her in ground support.

She listened to Kyle's voice, smooth and deep as

he talked to Glen Walsh, the other pilot in the air, and her disquiet once again rose up inside her.

"Hell to pay." What, exactly, had he meant by that? What did he intend to do? Take her out to the woodshed and spank her?

And what could possibly be gained by telling him the truth? He had no intention of quitting his military lifestyle. He didn't want a wife, didn't want a child, so what would he possibly do if he happened to discover this baby was his?

"Walsh...we've got a bogey at two o'clock." Kyle's voice, curt and filled with tension, exploded through her headset.

She sat up straighter, her heart thudding wildly in her chest. A bogey? Was Tamir about to make a move against Montebello? Had the simmering tensions finally exploded? Was an air strike imminent?

"There's another one at four o'clock...dusting the crops," Walsh replied, his voice also filled with the tension and anticipation of trouble.

Two planes from Tamir were apparently approaching Kyle and Glen. Joanna's first instinct was to scream for them to get away, to run from any encounter. Her heart crashed into her ribs as she realized Kyle was in danger.

And in that moment of fear, she realized her self-deception where he was concerned. She'd believed she had a firm hold on her emotions. She'd believed she could go to bed with him, enjoy his kisses, his caresses, and not get emotionally involved.

She'd thought she could spend time with him, learn little pieces of him, the nuances of the boy he had been and the man he had become, and not have her heart become involved with him. She'd been a fool.

She was in love with Kyle Ramsey. That knowledge only made her stronger in resolving that if he asked, she would never, could never, marry him. The only thing worse than being married to a military man was being married to a military man you loved.

Adrenaline rocked through Kyle as he looked first at his radar screen, then out the cockpit window. The screen showed there was a total of four Tamir fighter planes in the air approximately ten miles from where he and Glen were flying.

So far, they had not left Tamir air space and had made no aggressive moves. But Kyle was prepared, his body and mind ready for anything.

And he was relieved—relieved to have something else to think about besides Joanna and her surprising condition. He almost wished the Tamir planes would make a move of aggression so he could use his skills in venting his anger against the enemy.

Four to two, he thought to himself. A challenge, certainly, but Kyle had faced far worse odds and survived to tell the tales.

"It looks like they're just letting us know they are there," Glen transmitted.

"Yeah, well, if they leave their air space, they are gonna know we're here," Kyle replied.

For long, tension-filled moments, Kyle tracked the planes on his screen, waiting for them to suddenly

shoot out of Tamir air space and into Montebello
territory.

After ten minutes or so, the four blips on the radar
screen moved farther away, until they disappeared
altogether. "I guess we scared them off," Glen said
with a hoot of triumph.

"Looks that way," Kyle replied, the adrenaline
high slowly seeping out of him. "I think Sheik Kamal just wanted to let us know that he's aware of
our air patrols and is doing a little air patroling of
his own."

They bantered a little bit more, then fell silent. The
radar screen remained blissfully clear, and Kyle
found his thoughts once again turning to Joanna.

Pregnant. Joanna was pregnant. And he didn't believe her story about some mysterious Gary who was
the father of the baby. She hadn't been able to meet
his eyes as she'd said the name.

She'd been lying. Kyle felt it in his gut. He hadn't
forgotten that she'd told him none of the men at the
embassy acted like they even knew she was a
woman. Now she was trying to tell him that one of
those same men had dated her, slept with her, made
love to her? It just didn't wash.

Besides, according to her, she'd been a week or
two pregnant on the night he'd met her. He had a
little understanding of how these things worked, and
knew the odds of her knowing she was pregnant before meeting him was slim to none.

If there was a Gary and she'd slept with him a
week or two before she'd met Kyle, then there was

a fifty-fifty possibility that Kyle himself was the father.

He'd always been so careful about having protected sex, had never before taken a chance until that time with Joanna. That night, the last thing on his mind had been safe sex.

All he'd been interested in was making love to her as soon as they got into his hotel room. He'd just assumed that she was probably on the pill or whatever.

He had seen the signs, but had misread them. He'd thought she'd merely gained a little weight, thought he'd simply forgotten the size of her breasts. He'd noticed that she never ate breakfast, and occasionally on the way to work would nibble on a package of crackers that she kept in her purse. Morning sickness. Of course.

All the symptoms had been there, but none of it had hit home until he'd noticed the book lying on the coffee table in the living room. He'd picked it up, read the title, then everything had crashed together in his head.

And what was he going to do if he discovered the baby was his? Just walk away? Turn his back on Joanna and the child she carried?

He couldn't do that. He couldn't just walk away. He had a responsibility to them both. He hadn't intended to have a wife or a child, but if Joanna was pregnant with his baby, then of course he would do the right thing. He would marry her for the baby's sake.

However, before he did anything, he needed to find out what he could about this mysterious Gary and what exactly he intended to do if the baby was his.

Chapter 9

It was just after noon when Kyle got out of his taxi in front of the embassy, prepared to find the man Joanna had insisted was the father of her baby.

As he went through the security checks, his mind raced. He and Joanna had finished their shift at 2:00 a.m. They had barely spoken as she'd driven him home.

Once she had dropped him off, Kyle had tried to get some much-needed sleep, but sleep had remained elusive. Thoughts of the possibility of his impending fatherhood had whirled around in his head.

He recognized that the reality of the baby had not fully set in, that he hadn't fully comprehended the responsibilities that fatherhood entailed. The existence of the baby still didn't feel real to him.

He had been plagued by thoughts not only of the

baby, but of Joanna, as well. He was surprised to discover that the thought of her with another man, the idea of another man kissing her, touching her, making love to her, bothered him a great deal.

On the night he had met her, had she been kicking up her heels after breaking up with the mysterious Gary? Or had Gary broken up with her, and she had gone to the bar that night in order to prove her desirability to herself?

Neither scenario seemed right to Kyle. Most women, following a breakup of an intimate relationship, wanted to talk about it. Joanna had said and done nothing that night to indicate she had just gotten out of a relationship of any kind.

He'd finally fallen to sleep for a couple of hours, then had gotten up, determined to find out what the truth was where Joanna and her pregnancy were concerned. There was no point in him dwelling on the challenges of fatherhood if he truly wasn't the father of the baby she carried.

As he left the security checks, he headed for the one place he knew where gossip would run rampant, the most likely place for him to get answers he sought.

At this time of day the small embassy cafeteria was packed with people, some waiting in the food line, others crowded at the tables and still others just standing around chatting to each other.

Kyle took a tray and made his way through the line, his stomach rumbling with hunger despite the fact that he had more important things on his mind than eating.

He helped himself to a small salad, then got a serving of something that vaguely resembled Salisbury steak and mashed potatoes. After paying for his food, he stood and perused the various tables, seeking a group of people who looked most likely to be gossips.

Too bad gossips didn't wear hats or signs, so you'd know who to talk to when you wanted the scoop and who to avoid if you had a secret, he thought.

Although he knew it was sexist, he had a feeling that he would hear more gossip from a group of women than a group of men.

He spied a group of older women clustered together at one of the tables. They chattered like magpies among themselves, and Kyle had a feeling this was a likely place to start.

Seeing that there was an empty seat at their table, he headed directly for it.

"Good afternoon, ladies," he said, turning on his most charming smile. "Mind if I join you?"

"And why would we object to such a handsome thing like you sitting with us?" a silver-haired woman with bright blue eyes exclaimed, pulling out the empty chair next to her. "Take a load off, handsome. I'm Marge Winslow."

"Kyle Ramsey," Kyle replied, and nodded politely to each woman as she introduced herself to him. He then picked up his fork, deciding to bide his time and wait for a good opportunity to seek the answers he wanted.

For a few moments he simply ate, allowing the

conversation among the women to flow around him. Just from listening, he discovered that they were all secretaries from various departments and ate together every day.

He quickly learned that the daughter of one was getting married soon, and another's daughter was dating a hopeless loser. Two of the women were married, two were divorced and Marge was a widow.

When he saw that they were about to finish their meals, he finally broached the subject he needed to learn about. "Do you all know Joanna Morgan?" he asked. "She's a military attaché here."

"And a darling, sweet woman she is," Marge replied with a nod of her silvery head. "Why are you asking?" She gave him a sly grin. "Do I smell a budding romance?"

Kyle smiled sheepishly and lifted his shoulders in a gesture of helplessness. "I've just seen her around and think she's pretty. Do you know if she is seeing anyone in particular?"

"Joanna doesn't date," another of the woman replied. "She doesn't have time. That woman works longer hours than most of us put together. I've spent a little time with her—you know, coffee breaks and such—and I know she never goes out socially with men."

"But I heard she was seeing somebody who works here…somebody named Gary," Kyle said.

He watched as the women frowned and exchanged glances. "I don't know anyone here named Gary," Marge exclaimed.

"I do payroll," another woman said, "and I can

tell you for sure that nobody named Gary works at the embassy.''

"Somebody is pulling your chain, sugar," Marge said, and patted his arm.

"Yeah, I'd say somebody is definitely pulling my chain," Kyle replied, a swift jolt of anger surging up inside him.

"Say, honey," Marge said, "you don't have a daddy at home looking for a spicy relationship with a needy widow woman, do you?"

"I might have, but my mother tends to frown on that sort of thing," he replied.

"Ah, a pity," Marge said, her eyes twinkling.

She'd lied, Kyle thought. Joanna had lied to him. Even though he'd suspected at the time that she was spinning a story, the certainty that she'd lied to him filled him with ire.

"Thank you, ladies, for the information," he said as they began to check their watches and finish up last-minute bites.

"You won't go wrong hooking up with somebody like Joanna," one of the women said. "Everyone here thinks very highly of her. She's bright and beautiful, but also the sweetest woman in the world."

He nodded. The sweetest liar in the world, he mentally amended. As the women left the table, Kyle stood as well, no longer hungry except for an immediate confrontation with Joanna.

Moments later, as he sat in the back of a cab carrying him toward her house, he stewed in agitation. Why would she lie to him? Why hadn't she simply told him the truth—that the night they had shared, the night that had haunted him for months, had resulted in her pregnancy?

Was it because she truly believed he would be a horrible father? Kyle knew he'd be lying to himself if he didn't recognize that someplace deep inside he'd always feared just that. And that's why he had made the decision long ago not to become a father.

He'd had little of a role model from his own absentee father. Certainly he'd understood the fact that his dad had an important duty to fulfill, and that was why he had spent most of Kyle's childhood away from the family.

However, knowing the reasons why didn't mitigate the fact that Kyle had enjoyed little of his father's influence in his life. How could he possibly be a good father when he didn't know what that role required?

He shoved these thoughts aside. His father had done what he could, and Kyle would do the same. Hell, it must have been enough, for Kyle had certainly turned out all right.

As the cab pulled up in front of Joanna's house, Kyle prepared himself for battle. She might not want him as the father of her baby, but he *was* the father and she was just going to have to deal with that…and with him.

"Wait for me," he said to the cabbie. "I shouldn't be too long." He didn't intend to have a long, drawn-out argument with her. He just wanted to tell her what was to be done, then leave.

He knocked rapidly on the door, his anger radiating in the sharp staccato announcing his presence. He knocked three times before the door opened.

She stood before him, and it was obvious he'd awakened her. Clad in a short, turquoise terry robe, with her hair all tousled and her eyes slightly droopy with sleep, she looked achingly vulnerable and eminently touchable.

Kyle steeled himself against any soft feelings he might entertain for her. "We need to talk," he said, and pushed past her into the living room.

"Gee, come on in," she said dryly, and shut the door behind him. She walked across the room, her long shapely legs drawing his attention until she sat on the sofa and eyed him somberly. "So, what is so important that it couldn't wait until I picked you up for work later this afternoon?"

"Gary."

She visibly paled and cleared her throat with obvious nervousness. "Wha-what about him?"

"He doesn't exist." Kyle stared at her, daring her to continue to perpetuate her lie.

She sighed and stared at the carpeting just in front of where he stood. She didn't speak for a long moment, and Kyle wished he knew what was going on in her pretty head.

"What did you do?" she finally asked. "Go to the embassy and snoop around about my personal life?"

"That's exactly what I did."

Her gaze shot to his, and in the depths of her choc-olate-brown eyes he saw sparks of outrage. "How dare you! What gives you the right to do something like that?"

He held up a hand to halt whatever else she was going to say. "How dare *I*? How dare *you*. How dare you lie to me and make up some man as a pretend lover just so you don't have to tell me you're pregnant with my child."

His anger once again filled him. She had not only tried to deny him the right to be a father, but had also apparently intended to deny his child the right to a father. "You lied, Joanna. You looked me right in the eyes and lied to me."

She jumped up off the sofa, her eyes blazing with indignation. "What else should I have done? For goodness sakes, Kyle, you've made it abundantly clear to me that you don't want to be a father. I figured why tell you? Why burden you with what I knew you would only consider to be bad news?"

"Because it was my right to know," he retorted just as heatedly.

"Your right? You slept with me for a single night. Why should that give you any rights?" she exclaimed.

He narrowed his eyes and held her gaze without saying a word.

Her cheeks filled with color, and once again she averted her gaze from his. "Okay. You're right. I should have told you."

All the anger seemed to seep out of her and she once again sank down on the sofa, looking more defenseless and vulnerable than before. "I was just trying to do you a favor and not get you involved where you so obviously didn't want to be involved."

"It's too late for that now. I am involved." He

raked a hand through his hair, his anger still rich inside him.

He walked to the front door and pulled it open, then turned back to face her. "I've had since yesterday to contemplate what should be done if I'm the father. Now that I know for sure that I am, there's really only one logical solution."

She eyed him warily. "And what exactly do you think the solution might be?"

"It's quite simple. As soon as this mission is over, you'll go with me to the States and we'll be married." He didn't wait to see her expression or to hear her reply. He left through the door and returned to the waiting cab.

His mother would be thrilled and his father would probably even pat him on the back and congratulate him when they found out he was about to obtain not only a wife, but also a child.

Kyle frowned thoughtfully as the cab pulled away from her house. All in all, marriage to Joanna wouldn't necessarily be a bad thing.

He'd continue to fly missions, and she could set up a place for him to return to during downtime. He hadn't chosen to have a wife or to be a father, but it seemed fate had different plans for him. He would deal with the situation in the only way he could—by doing the right thing by her.

As far as Kyle was concerned, this was just another mission—one he hadn't volunteered for, but one where he would do his best to make it as successful as possible, like all the other missions he had ever undertaken.

* * *

The unmitigated gall of the man, Joanna thought as she watched the taxi disappear from her sight. He had some nerve to just appear on her doorstep, issue his command, then escape before he could reap any repercussions.

As if marrying him was any kind of a solution! As far as she was concerned there was no problem, therefore she had no need of his so-called solution.

She slammed her front door, and in the echo of that sound, she felt a pang explode in her heart. And in that explosion of pain, she recognized just what kind of monumental fool she was.

Somewhere in a teeny, tiny piece of her heart, she'd hoped that Kyle would take her in his arms, tell her that he realized he loved her, and promise that he would take a civilian job so he could come home to her and their baby every night.

But, of course, that hadn't happened. Kyle Ramsey had no intention of quitting the military, and his proposal certainly had nothing to do with love.

He was simply offering to do the "right thing." She knew exactly what he had in mind. He would install her at a military base—wherever he was currently stationed. He would fly off on missions and she would be left to cope with single parenting and loneliness. She could have all that without him, she thought ruefully.

She had no intention of marrying Kyle Ramsey. She wasn't about to repeat her miserable youth of rootlessness, didn't intend to subject her baby to a vagabond military existence. That lifestyle might be fine for some people, but she wanted something quite different for herself and her baby.

Not only was Kyle a man without dreams of his own, he was seemingly incapable of fulfilling the dreams she had for herself. And loving him only made marriage to him that much more of a foolish proposition.

Once again she sank down on the sofa, the ache in her heart expanding to fill each and every corner of her chest. How she wished her mother was here. How she wished she could talk to her mom, confide in her all her dreams, her qualms, all the pieces of herself she'd never shared with anyone.

She needed to talk to her about Kyle…about the fact that she loved a man who she suspected was incapable of forming any real attachment to anyone.

Rootless, adventurous, committed only to his job but nothing else… She'd teased him about being those things, but now it was nothing to tease or laugh about.

She was so torn, between the knowledge that Kyle had a right to be a part of her baby's life and the fear that he wouldn't be there for the child despite his best intentions. She was torn between wondering what was in the best interests of her baby—and how, in any way, did her own personal happiness play into that?

Kyle could be a part of the baby's life, but that didn't mean he had to be a part of hers, she realized. Surely they could work out an equitable arrangement that would satisfy not only both of them, but the child as well.

By the time she arrived at his apartment later that evening to pick him up for their shift at the base, she was armed and ready to take him on.

She waited until he was buckled into the passenger seat, then she pulled away from the curb and spoke for the first time since he'd entered the car. "I am not going to marry you."

"Don't be difficult, Joanna. Of course you're going to marry me," he replied curtly. "It's the reasonable thing to do."

"It is a positively unreasonable thing to do," she exclaimed. "You told me before that you couldn't imagine anything or anyone making you want to become a husband and a father."

"That was before," he replied, as if in that obscure statement lay all the answers.

She said nothing more until they arrived at the base and she was parked. Then she turned to look at him, trying to ignore how her heart rocked at the mere sight of him, how even now when she was trying to shove him firmly and resolutely out of her life, desire for him thrummed inside her.

It wasn't just a desire to be kissed by him, to feel his body against hers, it was a hunger for his love, a need to see inside his heart and discover where his dreams had been hidden. She steeled herself against these emotions.

"Kyle…let's be reasonable here. You don't want a wife and a child, and I don't need a husband."

His eyes looked more silver than gray as he gazed at her thoughtfully. "This isn't about what I want or what you need. This is about the baby…our baby."

She nibbled on her lower lip anxiously. She was suddenly tired, too tired to go on fighting with him. She had no idea how long their work would keep interaction between them necessary, and she didn't want to make things any more difficult than they already were.

"We can somehow work out a reasonable visitation schedule, if that's what you are worried about," she finally said.

He shook his head, firm resolve radiating from his features. "I don't want to visit my child, I want to be a part of his life. I want to be there to parent him."

"And how do you intend to do that?" The words exploded from her in frustration. Kyle's cool calm infuriated her and she wanted to scream. "How do you intend to parent him? Like your father parented you?"

His eyes glittered dangerously. "And just what was wrong with the way my father parented me?"

"He wasn't there. And his absence in your childhood left a hole inside your heart."

"You're obviously seeing things in my heart that aren't there," he countered, in a deadly calm tone that signaled to her that she was on dangerous ground.

Was it possible she'd misread the situation with his father? On the beach, she'd felt his hurt, a hurt he hadn't talked about, but one that had radiated out from him as he'd spoken of his father's absence during his childhood.

"Joanna, you're reading things that aren't there, probably because of your own experience," he said.

"I know you had a rough childhood, but not only was your father gone a lot, your mother wasn't there. Things will be different for our baby."

She frowned. He hadn't heard her. He hadn't accepted that she was rejecting his marriage proposal. "Kyle...this won't work. We can't get married."

"Why not?"

Because I love you, her heart cried out. Because you don't love me. Because in marrying you I will sacrifice every dream I ever had for myself. She bit her lip to keep those things from tumbling out of her mouth.

For the first time since he'd found the book about pregnancy on her coffee table, he smiled at her. "First and foremost, our marriage is the best thing we can do for our child."

His gaze lazily drifted down her body, warming her despite her reluctance. "Secondly, it's not like we can't stand each other. In fact, I can think of a lot of benefits where marriage is concerned."

Apparently he sensed her unwillingness to give in to him, her reluctance in agreeing to his marriage proposal. "I'll tell you what, let's take this one day at a time," he said, his smile fading.

He reached into his pocket and withdrew a small, black jewelry box. Joanna gasped in surprise. What had he done? Why was he making it all so difficult? Didn't he understand that him doing the "right thing" was absolutely the wrong thing for her?

"I took the liberty of picking this up after I left your place." He opened the box to reveal a beautiful white gold ring with a sparkling solitaire diamond.

He took the ring from the box and held it out to her. "Why don't we consider that, for the duration of the mission, we're officially engaged. You wear this ring and we take it one day at a time."

She gazed at the ring and felt that if she took it, if she wore it even for a brief time, it might suffocate her, squeeze to death all the dreams she'd ever had for her life.

Her gaze shifted from the ring to him. "But it's a ridiculous idea. I know that you are poor long-term material."

His eyes darkened. "Then I guess I'll just have to use our engagement time to change your mind about me." He held out the ring once again. "Take it…wear it. You owe it to our baby to at least do that much."

At that moment, a gentle fluttering occurred in her stomach. Although it was scarcely more than the beat of butterfly wings, or the whisper of a breath against a cheek, Joanna gasped and recognized it for what it was—the first stirring of life she'd felt physically.

"What's wrong?" Kyle asked, his voice edged with alarm.

"Nothing," she hurriedly said.

She touched her stomach, a wave of warmth and love and happiness surging up inside her. For the first time since the doctor had confirmed her pregnancy, she basked in the sweet pleasure of her condition.

She looked at Kyle. Filled up with love of their baby, she didn't want to argue anymore or increase the tension that already existed between them.

They still had to work together, interact with each

other on a daily basis. She didn't want to fight with him.

She took the ring from him and slid it on her finger. "One day at a time," she said softly. "But I'm not making any promises about marrying you."

He grinned in that sexy way that always made her feel a little bit shivery inside. "I'll just have to make sure that I make it impossible for you to say no to me."

She fought off a shiver at the thought of what his words implied. She was already far too vulnerable where he was concerned.

"We'd better get inside or we're going to be late," she murmured, needing some distance, some time to think without his presence overwhelming her senses.

He nodded and opened the car door to get out, and she did the same.

Neither of them spoke as they walked toward the building. The ring around Joanna's finger felt cold, alien, as if it didn't belong there. She thought of how different it might feel if it had been given with love and the promise of commitment.

But love and commitment hadn't been part of Kyle's proposal, she reminded herself. If she wasn't pregnant with his child there would be no proposal and no ring.

She would continue to work with Kyle. She would wear his ring and remain engaged to him. She would have his baby, but she was never going to make love to him again, and there was certainly no way she was ever going to marry him.

Chapter 10

Joanna sat on the ground with the warmth of the sun
on her shoulders. Around her the air was thick with
the scents of burgeoning spring—the rich smell of
the earth, the fragrance of new growth on the nearby
grapevines and grapefruit trees.

Sighing, she raised a hand and stared at the ring
on her finger. The diamond captured the sun's rays
and glittered brilliantly, as if imbued with the sparkle
of a million stars.

She'd been wearing the ring for almost three days
now and still it felt as alien and wrong as it had from
the first moment she'd slipped it on her finger.

During this time, Kyle had tried to get her to spend
her spare time with him. For the most part she'd
managed to put him off, pleading tiredness...
appointments at the embassy and other vague commitments.

The truth was, she was afraid to spend any time with him. She feared that he would look at her with those sexy gray, bedroom eyes of his, afraid that he might touch her just enough to weaken not only her knees but her resolve to keep her heart, her body and her soul distant from him.

Joanna sighed and focused her attention on the gravestone before her. Marie Madelena Morgan. Her mother. When she had passed away, Joanna's grandmother had requested that instead of her being buried at a military cemetery, her body would be sent back here—to her home. To the island of Montebello and her family.

Joanna's father had complied with the request, and so Marie Morgan now rested with the Voritelli family members who had passed on before her.

Joanna had awakened early that morning with two objectives in mind. Because it was not only her day off, but Kyle's day off as well, she was eager to get up and out of her house before he could call and try to set up time together.

Secondly, a heartfelt need had beat inside her—the need to come here, to the simple farm home where her mother had grown up and where Joanna's grandmama still lived.

Joanna had not stopped in at the house upon arriving, but had instead parked the car and walked directly here, to the small graveyard. It was set a short distance from the fruit trees and vines that provided her grandmama a simple, but steady living.

Joanna's mother's family had been on this land for almost a hundred years. Generations of her ancestors had lived in the plain ranch house where her grand-mama now lived.

The house was simple, without many of the amenities Joanna considered necessities, but it represented longevity and stability. Roots, she thought.

She closed her eyes and once again raised her face toward the warmth of the sun, wishing some of the heat could seep inside her and warm the places that felt as if they'd been cold forever.

How she wished she had been born and raised here. How she would have loved to have had the security of awakening every morning in the same bed in the same room, knowing that tomorrow would bring no unsettling changes.

Perhaps then she wouldn't be filled with such a deep yearning for that kind of security. Perhaps then she would have been able to accept what Kyle was offering her, and it would have been enough for her.

But it wasn't enough. And she didn't think it would ever be.

A soft rustling from someplace behind her drew her attention. She turned her head to see her grand-mama approaching.

As usual, despite the rising heat, Filomena Vori-telli was clad in a traditional long black skirt and a long-sleeved, white cotton blouse. Her salt-sprinkled dark hair was twisted into a heavy braid down her back.

She said not a word, but surprised Joanna by sinking down to sit by her side. Joanna had been to her mother's grave many times in the past three years, but never had her grandmama joined her here.

Joanna remained silent, knowing through experience that her grandmama would speak only when she was good and ready.

For a few minutes the two women sat side by side. The only sound was the rustle of a slight breeze through the leaves of the nearby trees and the call of birds from the sky overhead.

"There was a time when I couldn't come here." Filomena finally broke the silence, her dark gaze focused on the headstone that held her daughter's name. "For years the pain was simply too great for me to come here and speak to Marie. She was my only child, you know."

Filomena's pain radiated inside Joanna. She reached for the old woman's hand. It was the first time in her life Joanna had ever initiated physical contact with her grandmother, and she tensed, half expecting the gesture to be rebuffed.

But Filomena's hand gripped hers, her skin dry and leathery, but oddly comforting. "You are troubled. I can see it in your eyes." She turned to face Joanna, her raisin-brown eyes sharp and astute.

Joanna sighed, unsure how much to unburden to this woman she loved, but didn't feel she really knew. "I'm pregnant." The words escaped her lips before she even knew they had taken form in her mind.

She tensed, unsure what the elderly woman's reaction might be to the news. Filomena merely nodded, as if unsurprised at the announcement. She released her hold on Joanna's hand and continued to gaze at her. "And you are not happy about this?"

"No...I mean yes, I'm very happy about it," Joanna said quickly. She touched her stomach, love for the child within radiating through her, tension winging alongside as a vision of Kyle's face detonated in her mind. "I want this baby more than anything else in the world," she explained. "And I intend to be the absolute best mother in the whole wide world."

"And the father?"

Joanna felt the frown that immediately creased her forehead, but could do nothing to transform it. "I don't know, Grandmama." She sighed, and heard her turmoil pulsating in the expulsion of breath. "He wants to marry me."

"And you do not want to marry him?"

"I love him. I'd love to marry him...but he doesn't love me." The words sent a new shaft of pain searing through Joanna. "My heart says it doesn't matter, to go ahead and marry him for the baby's sake, but my head says no."

"Ah." Filomena returned her gaze to Marie's headstone.

"The most difficult thing a woman has to learn is when to listen with her head and when to listen with her heart." She pointed a bony finger toward the stone. "Your mother, she never learned to listen to anything but her heart."

Joanna tried to hide her surprise. Filomena never brought up the subject of Marie, a topic Joanna always hungered to discuss.

"She wasn't headstrong, she was heart strong," Filomena continued. She chuckled, the sound as dry and raspy as the thin skin of her hands. "The moment she met your father, her heart embraced him with a love so intense it frightened me for her."

Once again Filomena looked at Joanna. "Your father was a handsome charmer who seemed as taken with Marie as she was with him. When I saw the two of them together for the first time, I knew I had lost my daughter to him."

Filomena sighed. "I tried to tell her to take some time, not to move so fast, but there was no changing her mind where your father was concerned."

Again Joanna rubbed a hand across her lower abdomen, thinking of the young woman her mother had been and the pain Filomena must have felt when Joanna's father took Marie away from Montebello.

"It must have broken your heart when they left here to go live in the States," she said to the old woman.

Filomena looked surprised. "Broke my heart? No. It was impossible for me to harbor any pain in my heart when Marie was so filled with happiness and love. Besides, that's the natural way of life...that we release our children, allow them to build their own lives."

"But Father always told me you were against the marriage," Joanna replied.

"I was against them marrying so quickly, and when she died, I took out my grief against your father. It was wrong of me."

"I wish she was here right now," Joanna said softly.

"Ah, but part of her is here. Her spirit is in the

air that smells so sweet, in the gentle wind that whispers to me. And she is inside you.'' Filomena's gaze slowly took in each of Joanna's facial features. ''You are the image of her, and I see her heart shining from your eyes.''

A sense of peace radiated through Joanna at her grandmama's words, a peace she'd never before experienced concerning her mother.

''But I'll bet you wish now that you'd stopped her from marrying my father,'' Joanna said.

Filomena smiled, deepening the wrinkles on her nut-brown face. ''No. I wish she would have lived. I wish I would have had one more day with her. I wish she could have been here to raise and love you, but I would never wish to take away the tremendous happiness she felt during that year she had with your father.''

''He was good to her?'' Joanna was hungry not only to know the mother she'd never had, but also the father who had rarely been there for her.

Filomena's smile deepened and she looked up at the bright blue sky overhead. ''He was a besotted fool where she was concerned. Her letters to me were filled with the little things he did to make her happy, descriptions of presents he'd bought her and notes he'd written to her. He made my Marie incredibly happy.''

She directed her attention back to Joanna. ''It must have been difficult for him, to see you every day, to watch you grow to look so much like her. To tell the truth, it's always been difficult for me.''

This time it was her grandmama who reached for

her hand. "I have allowed my grief to keep me distant from you, and for that I am sorry. You are a celebration of Marie's life…and the child you carry is a joyous continuation of that celebration."

Filomena released her hand, and with a grimace, rose to her feet. "I need to get back to the house. I'm an old woman who has chattered too much." She took several steps, then turned back to Joanna.

"Only you can make the choice, Joanna. Only you can decide if it's best that you follow your heart or follow your head. Just be prepared to live with the consequences of whatever you choose." She turned and walked away, not offering a backward glance.

Joanna watched her go, then turned back to stare at the headstone. *It must have been difficult for him, to see you every day, to watch you grow to look so much like her.* Filomena's words whirled around in Joanna's head.

Did that explain her father's absences from her? Had he distanced himself from her because she looked so much like the woman he had lost? If that was the case, then it was sad, but it also soothed one of the aches that had always throbbed inside Joanna.

But her grandmama's parting words had only served to increase her confusion. Follow her heart? Or follow her head?

Again she gazed at the diamond ring on her finger. If she didn't marry Kyle, then she would be alone and raising a child.

If she married him she would be condemning herself to a military lifestyle, a husband often not home…a husband who didn't love her, but wanted to do the right thing by her.

She would never know if he had other women, would never have the stability, the roots, the kind of true, unconditional love that she sought.

What she would have were stolen moments of splendor when Kyle was home. She would have occasional nights of being held in his arms, of feeling his body pressed against hers.

She would know incredible joy…but would those moments of joy outweigh the anguish and heartache of being married to Kyle?

Kyle knew Joanna had taken the engagement ring under duress. He'd seen the rebellion in her eyes, had felt her opposition to the very idea of marrying him radiating from her pores.

And it bothered him. It bothered him that she didn't want him, had initially lied to keep him in the dark about her condition. And in the last three days, while she'd been wearing the ring, she'd grown more distant than ever.

He'd called her as soon as he'd gotten up that morning, but the phone had rung and rung without being answered. He knew that if she'd been there she would have picked it up, in case somebody from the embassy might be calling her.

With the day stretching out before him, he'd called a cab and had come to the marketplace not far from the palace. For the last several hours he'd been wandering, trying to figure out what was in Joanna's head.

He'd always believed women were relatively simple creatures. They liked sweet talk, dark chocolate and charm. He was happy to comply as long as they understood he wasn't in the market for a wife. Of all the women he'd dated or had relationships with, he'd known each one would have jumped at a marriage proposal.

Then there was Joanna. Joanna with the dancing dark eyes and sweet, full lips. Joanna with her quick wit and easy laughter. Joanna, who was carrying his child, had taken his ring, but according to her had absolutely no intention of marrying him.

Why not? What was wrong with him that she didn't want to share her life with him? Why didn't she see that it was the best thing to do for their child?

Kyle had no illusions about his feelings for Joanna. It wasn't as if he was in love with her or anything. He was smart enough to know that she had become a challenge to overcome, a mission to accomplish, and he'd never been unsuccessful when facing a challenge or a mission.

He stopped at one of the bazaar booths that held an array of scarves, his attention captured by a particular length of silk that was exactly the rich brown of Joanna's eyes.

He could easily imagine that swath of gossamer material around her neck, against the olive tones of her skin. He could also easily imagine her pulling that piece of cool silk down the length of his naked body, then him doing the same to her. It was a vision that instantly produced a wealth of heat inside him, an ache for her that, as always, astonished him.

It had been exactly thirteen days since he'd sat in Nigel Templeton's office waiting for the military attaché to arrive. It had been thirteen days since Kyle had been reunited with the woman who had walked out on him in the middle of the night, leaving him filled with questions and haunted by her memory. He frowned, wondering why thirteen days with Joanna hadn't been enough.

He bought the scarf, then left the marketplace and took a cab back to his apartment. During the ride he idly ran his fingers over the smooth, cool material, his thoughts consumed by Joanna.

In the past three days, since giving her the ring, he hadn't touched her, kissed her or made love to her. There had been a forbidding distance between them that he hadn't known how to breach. It was as if the engagement ring, instead of bringing them closer, had driven them further apart.

He yearned for the way things had been before he'd discovered she was pregnant with his baby. They had shared an easy camaraderie, plenty of laughs and lovemaking that others would envy. He wanted that again…with her.

As the cab pulled through the Ramsey Enterprises lot toward the apartment building, Kyle felt a sinking sensation in the pit of his stomach as he saw a familiar dark luxury car parked out front.

His father's car.

Kyle leaned forward and tapped the cabbie on the shoulder. "I've changed my mind." He gave the man Joanna's address, then sat back once again.

He wasn't ready for his father, wasn't mentally

prepared to face the confrontation he knew was waiting. He had enough on his mind with Joanna.

She wasn't home when the cab driver let him off, so he sat on her front porch and waited for her. Around him the sounds of neighborhood living filled the air.

He could hear the whoops and laughter of children playing somewhere in the distance, and the whine of a Weed Eater. A dog barked, short yips that implied excitement. They were comfortable sounds...the noises of a home.

He hadn't been lying when he'd told Joanna that marriage wouldn't be all bad. Aside from the pleasure of their lovemaking, he knew she would build them a home wherever he was stationed.

She would take the sterile military housing and transform it into something warm and wonderful, a place that would welcome him each time he returned.

They could build a good life together despite the fact that it wasn't exactly what either of them had envisioned for themselves.

Checking his wristwatch, he wondered where she could be. Yesterday when they'd left the military compound she hadn't mentioned anything about appointments or commitments for the day. He hoped nothing had happened.

Their shift had ended late the night before. It had been after midnight when Joanna had dropped him at his apartment. He suddenly realized he didn't even know if she'd arrived home safely.

A niggle of fear shot through him. He knew women had miscarriages. But surely if she'd been experiencing cramping or bleeding, she would have called him.

Or would she?

He hated to admit it, but he wasn't at all sure that she would call him or come to him if any problem arose. She trusted him enough to have sex with him, but didn't trust him in her heart, and that bothered him.

He sighed in relief when he saw her car approaching the house. As she parked in the driveway, he stood to greet her.

"Kyle," she exclaimed, obviously surprised to see him. "What are you doing here?" She started up the sidewalk toward him.

He met her halfway and pulled her into his arms. "Isn't a man allowed to pop in just for the pleasure of seeing his fiancée?"

He'd hoped to see her eyes light with pleasure at his words, but instead they darkened, as if what he'd said caused her some sort of pain. She stepped out of his embrace to unlock her front door.

She was dressed casually, in a sleeveless, coral-colored dress and sandals. The dress had no structure to it, but fell loose and flowing to her ankles. The color did dynamite things to her skin and emphasized the sparkling darkness of her eyes.

"Where have you been?" he asked lightly as she ushered him into the living room.

"I went to visit my grandmama and to my mother's grave."

Instantly, Kyle had the desire to take her in his

arms and comfort her. "Your mother is buried here on Montebello?" he asked instead.

She nodded and sank down on the sofa. "My father agreed to have her buried here in the family cemetery."

Kyle sat next to her and breathed in her scent, that intoxicating fragrance that never failed to stir him. He reached out and touched a tendril of her silky hair. "Are you all right?"

Her responding smile held a touch of surprise at his question. "Yes, I'm fine. I had a nice visit with both my grandmama and my mother."

"I'm glad," he replied. "Oh, I almost forgot." He grabbed the paper sack that held the scarf. "I was at the marketplace earlier and I bought you a surprise." He handed her the sack.

"A surprise?" Her face lit with pleasure, and Kyle suddenly wished it was something more than a mere silk scarf. He wished it was a sackful of diamonds, or a thousand sweetly scented wildflowers.

She pulled it out of the sack and held it up to her cheek. "Oh, Kyle...it's beautiful," she exclaimed.

"No, you are," he countered, the words falling from his lips as he gazed at the chocolate-colored scarf against her beautiful silky skin.

Her cheeks flamed with color and she stood and moved away from the sofa, as if suddenly uncomfortable with their proximity. "Thank you. I appreciate you thinking of me."

He stood and followed her, not wanting to allow any distance between them. "And who else would I think about besides the woman I intend to marry?"

He placed his hands on her shoulders, wanting to draw her close and feel her heartbeat against his own. He wanted to kiss those luscious lips that had parted just slightly at his touch. But he felt her shoulders stiffen, sensed an unyielding rigidity in her body.

"Joanna...tell me what's going on in that pretty head of yours," he said softly, refusing to drop his hands although he knew she wanted him to. "Ever since I gave you that ring, you've grown more and more distant."

He was forced to drop his hands when she once again moved away from him. "It's a big transition to make, Kyle." Her dark eyes studied him soberly. "Even though we're engaged, we really don't know each other very well at all."

He smiled and held her gaze. "I think there are some areas where we know each other very well."

"That's just it, Kyle," she exclaimed with more animation than she'd shown since he arrived. "We can't spend the bulk of our time in bed."

"Why not?" he asked with a teasing grin.

She emitted a small, dry laugh and shook her head ruefully. "You are utterly incorrigible."

"Does this mean I shouldn't sweep you up in my arms, carry you into the bedroom and make wild, passionate love to you?"

He thought he saw just a whisper of longing in her eyes, there only a moment, then gone. He tried to tamp down the responding flicker of desire that ignited inside him, knowing instinctively that wasn't what she needed from him at the moment.

"It's just that I'm so confused," she finally said

softly. She looked up at him, her eyes dark pools of misery. "I'm afraid that if I marry you, it will be a mistake. And I'm afraid if I don't marry you, it will be a mistake. We really don't know each other well at all, Kyle. How can we be sure this is going to work?"

He reached out and touched her cheek softly, gently. "Joanna, you know as well as I do there are no guarantees, but we owe it to our baby to try." Her eyes merely grew darker, and frustration battled with his desire for her.

Stepping back from her, he raked a hand through his hair. "How can we get to know one another when you avoid me whenever you can?" he asked. Guilt raced across her features and her eyes refused to meet his. "Come to dinner tonight at my place," he said.

Her gaze flew to his, mistrust evident in the shining depths. He laughed, for the first time easily able to read her mind. "No, I'm not inviting you over for an evening of seduction, although I'd be lying if I didn't say the idea appealed to me. But the truth is my father is in town. Come and break bread with us."

Kyle didn't realize he'd been holding his breath until she nodded affirmatively and relief washed over him. "Great. I'll send a car for you around six."

"I can drive myself," she protested.

"No," he replied, the memory of his fear that something might have happened to her still knocking around inside him. "From now on I'll drive us to work and get you back home safe and sound. I don't want you driving the streets at all hours of the night, all alone.''

Again her eyes flickered with surprise. "Okay," she agreed. "But if you want me to be ready by six, then I need to start getting ready." She looked at her watch, then back at him.

He knew it was a not-so-subtle hint that she wanted him to leave. "All right, I'll get out of your hair." He leaned forward and kissed her on the forehead, then turned and left the house.

It was only when he stepped outside that he realized he had no way home. He'd come in a cab and had let it go because he'd hoped he might spend the afternoon in Joanna's bed.

It had been a fool's hope, especially with the way things had been going between them for the past several days.

He thought of going back into her house and calling for a cab, but decided to walk until he found an establishment that had a phone. The longer he took to get home, the less time he'd have to spend alone with his father.

And of course, that was the reason he'd invited Joanna to dinner—because she would make a perfect buffer between the two headstrong men. It had nothing to do with anything else, he told himself firmly.

It had nothing to do with the fact that in the past three days, as she'd drawn further and further away from him, he'd felt a sense of panic that he didn't understand.

Chapter 11

Joanna had no idea why she was so nervous, but as she sat in the back of the car that was taking her to Kyle's, her nerves jangled with anxiety. It was crazy, but she was every bit as nervous as when she'd gone to eat dinner with King Marcus and Queen Gwendolyn.

Kyle's father. Somehow meeting Edward Ramsey made the engagement, the baby and her relationship with Kyle feel that much more substantial.

The problem was, she still wasn't sure what, exactly, she wanted her relationship with Kyle to be in the future. She loved him—that was the one thing she was certain of—but she was realistic enough to know that sometimes love wasn't enough. Especially when only one of the people in the relationship was in love.

She closed her eyes and leaned her head back, knowing that whether she decided to walk away from Kyle or not, she would never fully recover from the heartache of loving him.

And she did love him. She'd never felt this way about anyone before in her life. His laughter sang in her heart, his touch burned her soul, and the gentle caring he'd shown her two hours earlier had nearly been her undoing.

She thought of the tenderness in his eyes as he'd told her he didn't want her driving alone anymore, the concern that had colored his voice when he'd asked about her visit to her mother's grave.

She could accept his passion more easily than she could his tenderness and compassion. That, if anything, would weaken her resolve not to marry him.

Opening her eyes, she sat up straight in the seat and drew several deep, long breathes in an attempt to ease her nerves. She had to commit soon, for the uncertainty was growing too enormous to bear.

She had to decide one way or the other. Either she made it clear to Kyle that they positively, absolutely didn't have a future together, or she fully gave herself to him without any more reservations. Drifting along in this indecision was making her crazy.

A sweet fluttering stirred deep inside her, and she knew it was the new life within. Not only did she have to think about what was best for her, she had to consider what was best for her child, as well.

She thought of the evening ahead and hoped desperately that Kyle hadn't told his father she was pregnant. Kyle's pressure on her to marry him was quite enough; she didn't want to add any additional pressure from a prospective grandfather.

Grandfather. If she married Kyle, her baby would not only have a mother and a father, but a large extended family as well.

Truth be told, it had been mainly curiosity that had made her agree to the dinner. Each time Kyle had spoken of his father she'd heard the underlying tension, felt stress radiating from him.

She couldn't believe that Kyle was still holding a grudge against his father because Edward Ramsey hadn't allowed his son to join the navy before he came of age. That had been years ago, and that breach should have been healed through love, maturity and time.

But she hadn't mistaken the hostility in Kyle each time he'd spoken of his father, and she was interested to meet the man who had raised the man she loved.

By the time the driver pulled up before the apartment building, Joanna's nerves were positively screaming with anxiety.

The driver, a young man with the coloring of a native, who had told her he drove for Edward whenever the businessman was in town, opened the door to usher her out. "Here you are, safe and sound," he said. "Mr. Kyle told me he would have my head on a platter if I didn't get you here in one piece."

She smiled. "Then it looks like you get to keep your head. I'll tell him you were a cautious driver and also very courteous."

He nodded with a happy smile and she headed for

the building, leaving him standing by the car as if in anticipation of the next time he might be needed.

As she stepped into the elevator, she smoothed the material of her beige linen skirt, hoping the casually elegant outfit was appropriate for dining with her fiancé's father.

She touched the silk scarf she wore at her neck. The dark brown of the scarf complemented the pale beige dress. She'd been deeply touched that Kyle had thought of her while he'd wandered the marketplace.

She drew a deep breath as the elevator came to a halt and the doors slid open. It was ridiculous to be so nervous, ridiculous to care what Edward Ramsey thought of her. After all, there was no guarantee he would have anything at all to do with her future.

A tall, handsome young man with reddish-brown hair answered her knock. She instantly recognized him as Tyler Ramsey, Kyle's youngest brother.

"Wow," he exclaimed, his green eyes holding a teasing friendliness as he took her hand and drew her into the foyer. "Please tell me you have a single sister at home who looks just like you."

"Sorry," she said with a laugh as he led her into the living room. "I'm an only child."

"Rats," he replied. "My big brother always has all the luck. By the way, I'm Tyler…the youngest of the Ramsey brood."

"I'm Joanna Morgan. It's nice to meet you."

"Ah, I see my brother is attempting to practice his dubious charm." Kyle stepped into the living room, clad in tight worn jeans, a short-sleeved gray dress shirt and a barbecue apron.

"Actually, I don't find his charm dubious at all," Joanna replied with a teasing smile.

"Ha!" Tyler grinned triumphantly. "Then I must be improving."

"Don't encourage him, Joanna," Kyle replied with a grin of obvious fondness at his brother. "He's a rake and a rascal."

"Following in his big brother's footsteps, no doubt," Joanna replied dryly.

Tyler laughed and threw an arm around her shoulder. "I think I'm going to like this woman," he said. "Come on into the kitchen, Joanna, where you can watch your fiancé use his culinary skills to whip up dinner."

They entered the large attractive kitchen, and Tyler led her to a stool at the work island, where Kyle had apparently been preparing a large salad. She didn't know how she felt about the fact that Kyle had told his brother of their engagement.

"Is there anything I can do to help?" she asked as she sat on a tall stool next to Tyler.

"No, I think I've got it all under control," Kyle replied, moving to the opposite side of the island and grabbing a knife to resume cutting up green peppers for the salad. "It's nothing elaborate, just steak, salad and baked potatoes."

"As much as I hate to admit it, Kyle makes the best steaks in the entire world," Tyler said.

Kyle grinned at Joanna, his gaze soft and warm. "The secret is in the marinade sauce."

"And what is in your sauce?" she asked.

Kyle leaned over the island and touched the tip of

her nose. "Now, if I told you that, it wouldn't be a secret."

"Maybe you'll have better luck than we've had in finding out his ingredients," Tyler said. "Mom, Dad, Jake and I have been trying to get him to tell us for years. But he refuses to divulge his secrets."

"Speaking of your family, I thought you said your father was here," Joanna said to Kyle.

"He'll be here. He ran to his office, but will be back anytime," Kyle explained.

"He's going to positively be blown away when he hears the news of Kyle's engagement," Tyler exclaimed.

"You haven't told him yet?" Joanna asked curiously.

Kyle shook his head. "He was already gone by the time I got back here this afternoon. I told Tyler that we dated about four months ago, when I was here before, and that we picked up where we left off when I returned."

Gratefulness fluttered through her. She could tell by his careful words and the look on his face that he wanted her to know he hadn't told his brother they'd had a one-night fling that had resulted in an unexpected pregnancy and a sudden engagement.

"And it's about time my eldest brother decided to get married and settle down," Tyler said. "I'm most thankful that his wedding will get Mom off my back at least for a little while."

Kyle laughed and threw a piece of carrot at him. At the same moment they heard the sound of the front door opening, then closing.

"Hello?" a deep voice called out.

"In the kitchen, Dad," Tyler shouted. Kyle continued to cut vegetables, and Joanna steeled herself, unsure what to expect from the man who made Kyle so tense.

Edward Ramsey entered the kitchen and immediately filled it with the same kind of energy Joanna always felt when Kyle came into a room. It was also impossible not to notice that the firstborn son was merely a younger, more physically fit version of the older man.

Edward's hair was more gray than brown, and he was stout rather than lanky, but his facial features instantly told of the paternal connection to Kyle.

"Well, well. I didn't realize we had a guest." He nodded to Kyle and Tyler and approached Joanna with a friendly smile. "Edward Ramsey," he said, and held out his hand to her.

She returned his smile, noting that his eyes were the exact same shade of gray as Kyle's. "Joanna Morgan," she replied, as her hand was encompassed by his bigger one in a handshake.

"My fiancée," Kyle added.

Edward stared at his son in shock, then looked back at Joanna and smiled widely. "Well...well, that's wonderful news," he exclaimed, sounding pleased despite his obvious surprise. "Have you spilled this little bombshell to your mother, Kyle?"

"No, Major, we've been playing it rather low-key," Kyle replied.

Edward Ramsey's eyes darkened a shade as he gazed at his eldest son, then he smiled once again at

Joanna. "She'll be thrilled, as I am." He tugged at the tie around his neck. "And now, if you'll excuse me for a moment, I'll go get out of this monkey suit and into more comfortable clothing. Then we can chat and get better acquainted."

"You know he hates it when you call him Major," Tyler chided softly when the older man had left the room.

Kyle grinned. "I know, but things wouldn't be normal around here if I didn't get under his skin just a little bit." He turned his grin on Joanna. "You want something to drink? It's going to be about half an hour before we eat."

"No thanks, I'm fine," she replied, again wondering at the relationship between Kyle and his father.

"Well, I'm ready for a beer," Tyler said, and headed for the refrigerator. "What about you, Kyle?"

"No thanks, I'm on fly duty early in the morning."

"Yeah, what's up with that?" Tyler popped the tab on his beer can and sat once again on the stool next to Joanna's. "Dad mentioned that you told him you're working all kinds of weird hours. What's going on?"

Kyle set the finished salad aside. "If I told you, baby brother, then I'd have to kill you."

"Ah, one of those top secret deals."

Joanna listened with interest as the two brothers caught up on each other's lives. There was something comforting in the way the two men teased each other, their affection for one another apparent.

She realized again that if she married Kyle, she would not only be gaining a husband, but a whole family—a mother- and father-in-law and two brothers-in-law. She would have a place in their lives, in their hearts.... She would finally have a family. And her baby would have uncles as well as grandparents who would love and indulge a new baby.

It was a compelling reason to marry the man who, at the moment, was chatting with his brother while he kept one eye on the broiling steaks.

Within minutes Edward had rejoined them in the kitchen. They all helped place the food on the table, then sat down to eat. "So, have you two set a date yet?" Edward asked.

"Not yet," Joanna replied. "We have some things to finish up here, then are planning on going back to the States and will probably get married there."

"Joanna works at the embassy and is in charge of a project she wants to finish up," Kyle explained. He didn't explain the nature of the project or that he was working on the same thing.

Joanna knew he didn't want to prompt more questions that might compromise the secrecy of their current mission.

"Then you probably know Ambassador Templeton," Edward exclaimed. Joanna nodded and Edward continued, "A great man and one hell of a poker player." Edward smiled. "He can bluff better than any man I've ever met."

Joanna laughed. "Somehow that doesn't surprise

me about him. He's a wonderful man and it's been a privilege for me to work with him."

Edward turned his attention to his eldest son. "How are you doing, Kyle? Is the military keeping you busy? The news reports indicate there is some tension here in Montebello."

As the men discussed the current political atmosphere, Joanna carefully watched Kyle and his father. There might be tension in Montebello, but there was also tension between the two men right here at the dining table.

Although Kyle spoke to his father civilly, there seemed to be a subtle, underlying anger in his tone and in the rigidity of his body language.

Joanna knew that Edward felt it, and she also sensed a quiet desperation in him. It was the desperation of a man trying to connect in a meaningful way with his firstborn son.

She hadn't imagined the stress that colored Kyle's voice each time he spoke of his father. She didn't know what had caused their troubled relationship, but she did wonder how the resulting baggage would affect Kyle's ability to be a good father.

Touching her stomach, she realized she was as confused as ever concerning her decision whether to marry Kyle or not. Seeing the way he interacted with his father troubled her, adding to the list of other reasons she shouldn't marry him.

After dinner, Kyle insisted his father and brother leave the dishes for him and Joanna to take care of. The two men returned to the living room, leaving Kyle and Joanna alone in the kitchen.

"My father and my brother have known you for only a little over an hour and already they adore you," Kyle said as he wrapped his arms around her.

"I like them both," she replied, her heart pumping faster at their closeness. Why was it the simplest touch from him created such warmth, caused such intense pleasure to course through her? *Because you love him.* The answer came unbidden to her mind. "And I liked your steak. Tyler was right, you are a master steak cooker."

"You want to know what I like?" he asked, his voice husky and his eyes silvery with heat.

"What?" she asked in turn, her chest constricting as if there was not enough oxygen in the room. When he looked at her with those mesmerizing eyes, when his voice was low and husky, desire didn't build slowly inside her, but rather rocked through her in full-blown splendor.

"I like the fact that you're wearing the scarf I bought for you." He touched the silk at her neck, one finger stroking the sensitive skin just above it. She knew she should move out of his embrace, but her legs refused to listen to her head.

"Want me to tell you what my fantasy was when I bought this scarf?"

At that moment, Tyler and Edward laughed, breaking the spell Joanna had momentarily fallen into. She stepped out of Kyle's embrace. "No, I don't want to know what your fantasy was when you bought it." She grabbed several plates from the table, aware of his hungry gaze still lingering on her. "And stop looking at me that way or we'll never get these dishes done,'' she exclaimed.

He laughed. ''Okay, dishes first, but I know you'd like my fantasy.''

Yes, she would. Merely imagining what his fantasy might be had her weak in the knees and dry in the mouth. And he knew it. The satisfied smile on his lips told her he knew exactly what he did to her.

But was it enough? Would the fact that they would share incredible sex whenever he was at home be enough to sustain her during the days and weeks and months that he wouldn't be?

Could she live with the knowledge that he loved making love to her, but didn't love her? That she could possess his body but would never, ever possess his heart? Unsure of what the answers were, she shoved the questions out of her head.

When the kitchen was clean and everything back in order, she and Kyle rejoined his brother and father in the living room.

''So, tell me, Joanna, did you grow up here in Montebello?'' Edward asked.

''Joanna was a military brat, like we were,'' Kyle explained. Again Joanna was aware of a difference in his tone as he spoke to his father. There was a distinct edge to his voice and a whisper of something lost in his eyes.

Again she wondered at what negative forces existed between father and son and how they might affect Kyle's ability to be a good father.

Joanna and Edward visited, her telling him superficially about her childhood and the different bases and states where she had lived. He, in exchange, told her a little bit about Ramsey Enterprises and his wife.

They chatted for another hour, then Joanna murmured that she really needed to get home, as they had an early shift the next morning.

She'd assumed the same driver who had brought her would take her home, but Kyle insisted on driving her himself. "I like your family," she said once they were in the car and on their way to her house.

"Yeah, they're all right," he agreed easily.

"Your brother is a real charmer, and it's obvious your father loves you very much."

"Yeah, right," he said a bit dryly.

She looked at his handsome features in the glow from the dash. "Why are you so angry with him?" she asked softly.

"With who?"

"With your father."

He flashed her a surprised glance, then frowned and refocused out the car window. "I'm not angry with him," he replied, but his terseness told her otherwise.

"Kyle, please…talk to me," she said, wanting to understand, needing to understand what was going on inside the man she loved. "It's obvious there's something happening between you and your father. Tell me what's in your heart."

"There's nothing to talk about," he said as he pulled into her driveway. His tone was implacable, and it was at that moment that Joanna realized she was not going to marry him.

Not only did he not love her, but she realized now

he would never be able to share with her, to give up pieces of himself. He didn't trust her.

He shut off the engine and turned to gaze at her, his eyes lit with what had become a familiar, evocative light. "Now, do you want me to tell you about my fantasy with your scarf?"

Her heart ached as the knowledge of the decision she'd just made ripped through her. She would never know life as Kyle's wife. After tonight she would never again feel the breathtaking wonder of his body against hers, know the beat of his heart mirroring her own, taste the heat of his splendid kisses. After tonight...

She realized she'd made another split-second decision. She wanted one more night with him before she said her final goodbye.

"Instead of telling me about your fantasy, why don't you come inside and show me?" she said, her voice husky as it always was when she thought of making love with Kyle.

His eyes flared with hunger and he unfastened his seat belt, then leaned forward to capture her mouth with his. Instantly, tears rose up inside her, burning her eyes. She fought them, not wanting to have to explain to him that they were there because she was giving herself the gift of him one final time.

When he broke the kiss, they got out of the car. He placed an arm around her shoulders as they walked to the front door. As she unlocked it and started to step inside, he pulled her back against him, his eyes searching hers intently.

"Are you sure you want me to come in?" he

asked. And she only loved him more for giving her an opportunity to change her mind. But she didn't want to change her mind. Finally, for the first time in two weeks, she felt clearheaded and certain in the decisions she had made.

She didn't answer him verbally, but instead took him by the hand and drew him through the living room and into her bedroom, where moonlight spilled across the windowsill and lit the room with a faint glow.

Without saying a word, he pulled her to him and with deft fingers untied the scarf and lay it on the bed, then wrapped his arms around her and eased down the zipper of her dress.

As he was doing so, her fingers worked the buttons of his shirt, and when they were all undone, and it fell open, she slid her palms across his hard, muscled chest.

"It feels like it's been forever since I held you in my arms," he growled.

"It's been less than a week," she replied as her dress fell to the floor.

"A week can feel like an eternity."

And eternity without him would feel like hell, she thought, tears once again rising up inside her. As he pulled her down on the bed, she closed her eyes, fighting the tears that begged to be released.

She kept her eyes closed as he gently removed her panty hose, then her underclothing. He left her side only a moment and she heard his jeans fall to the floor, then he was back next to her, his naked body hot and hard against hers.

He drew the silky scarf down the length of her nakedness, the smooth, cool material tantalizing her flesh and shooting chills of pleasure throughout her.

"This is what my fantasy was," he whispered, his eyes silver in the pale moonlight.

And her deepest, sweetest fantasy was that he would tell her he loved her. But she knew that would remain an elusive, unfulfilled fantasy, would never become a reality.

Each stroke of his fingers, every kiss he gave her, every single touch between them seemed more intense than ever, and she knew it was because it was the very last time she would experience making love with Kyle.

When she could stand his touch no more, when she felt as if she would shatter if he caressed her one more time, she took the scarf from him and returned the pleasure.

Each moan that escaped him, every heated gaze, each sigh of her name she captured as a memory indelibly seared into her heart.

She would never again hear him moan with pleasure, never again see those beautiful gray eyes look at her with such savage hunger, and she would never again hear her name spoken with such tenderness, such desire.

She swirled the scarf down the length of him, following with her lips, wanting to make his pleasure as intense as her own.

His fingers tangled in her hair, and again her name escaped him, spoken so sweetly it revived her tears.

Never again.

The dreadful words went around and around in her head, a keening of sorrow that cried inside her. Never again would she make love to him, and after these precious moments in time, she had to tell him that she wasn't going to marry him.

But not now...not yet. First she needed to dwell in his arms for as long as possible, feel the magic that was always there when they made love...pretend that for just this moment he loved her as deeply, as profoundly as she loved him.

As if somehow he knew that this would be their last time together, he moved with an aching slowness, a breathtaking leisure that merely served to increase her pleasure...and her sadness.

By the time he finally entered her, tears fell soundlessly down her cheeks. She knew the tears were because she feared she couldn't live without him, yet knew she was going to have to do just that.

Chapter 12

"Eagle One to base," Kyle radioed. "I'm coming in."

"Eagle One, you're cleared for landing," Joanna's voice replied.

Kyle smiled. He'd been smiling from the moment he'd awakened that morning with Joanna in his arms. She'd been so warm and sweetly pliant against him, and as he'd watched dawn's light kiss her features, he'd felt a contentment he'd never known before.

Remembering their lovemaking not only made his smile deepen, but also set aflame a warmth in his groin. She had been so passionate the night before, giving with the same generosity as he'd given her.

Yes, there was nothing better than waking up with a snuggly warm, sweet-smelling woman in your arms, he thought. There was nothing better than waking up with a woman like Joanna in your arms.

Last night had been more than magnificent with her. He'd felt as if she'd finally dropped all her defenses and come to him with an openness, an intensity that had stolen his breath away.

He whistled a cheerful melody as he readied himself for landing. It had been another beautifully clear day, with no threats from Tamir to worry about. And he had spent the better part of the day basking in the warmth and pleasure of the night before.

If there had been any blight at all on the evening, it had been those hours spent with his father during and after dinner. As always, Kyle had felt the weight of his dad's disappointment in him.

Joanna had asked him why he was so angry with his father, and Kyle didn't know how to tell her he wasn't angry, he just dreaded the conversation he knew his father had come to Montebello to have with him.

Edward would ask him yet again to join the family business; Kyle would decline and feel his father's deep disappointment and frustration. Kyle would feel guilty and that guilt would produce anger. It was a vicious cycle the two men had endured for far too long.

Kyle didn't understand why his father was disappointed that he had chosen the same profession Edward had once chosen. Why couldn't his dad be proud that Kyle was following in his footsteps with his military career?

As the landing strip came into view, Kyle shoved all thoughts of his father and Joanna from his mind, focusing only on the task of getting his plane down safely.

A few minutes later he got out of the plane and headed for the operations room. It was just after two in the afternoon and he was hoping he could talk Joanna into going out for an early dinner.

She'd been unusually quiet that morning as they'd gotten up and dressed and he'd driven them to work in the car he'd rented. But he assumed she'd been quiet because it had been early and they'd gotten to sleep late.

By this evening, the short night would catch up to her. She was pregnant and probably required more sleep. He'd take her out for a good meal, then drive her back to her place and insist she go to bed early.

She stood with her purse, ready to leave, when he walked into the operation room. He kissed her on the forehead, then swept past her to change out of his flight suit.

When he was ready, they left the building and headed toward where his rental car was parked. "Tired?" he asked her.

"A little," she replied, her body language and facial features exhibiting not only weariness, but also more than a touch of stress.

"How about we go get something to eat, then I'll take you back to your place and you can have an early night?"

"If you don't mind, could you just take me home?" she asked as they reached his car.

He wanted to protest, to tell her that she needed to eat, that he wanted to see more of her than a drive

to work, then home. But he felt her weariness and
knew she probably needed to get home and rest.

"Sure," he agreed, deciding that maybe he could
hang out at her house while she napped, then they
could get something to eat together later.

They indulged in small talk on the way to her
house, speaking of the mission, the pilots and the fact
that there had been no show of force from Tamir.

"Maybe the passing of time is easing tensions,"
he said thoughtfully.

"As long as both King Marcus and Sheik Ahmed
are missing their sons, I don't think anything will
ease," she replied. "The search team still hasn't
found Prince Lucas's body, and Sheik Rashid Kamal
still hasn't been found."

"I just hope everything stays calm," Kyle replied.

She didn't answer and silence stretched between
them as he parked in her driveway. "Kyle, we need
to talk," she said then.

He grinned. "I thought that's what we've been
doing." His smile fell away as he saw the somber
darkness of her beautiful eyes. "What's wrong,
Joanna?"

"Come inside. I don't want to have this discussion
in the middle of my driveway."

He followed her up the walk to her front door,
dread rolling around in his stomach. What was going
on? Why did her eyes suddenly radiate such sadness?

She didn't speak again until she'd dropped her
purse on the coffee table, then turned to face him.
"Kyle, I've been doing nothing but thinking for the

past week, and I've come to a decision that affects us both."

"You want me to buy more silk scarves," he said in an attempt to alleviate the tension that suddenly filled him up and crackled in the air between them.

"Please, no jokes." There was a bleakness in her expression, a pain radiating from her eyes that turned his tension to fear.

"Joanna, what's going on?"

She sat heavily on the sofa, as if unable to remain standing. As he watched, she pulled the engagement ring off her finger and placed it on the coffee table before her. "I can't wear that any longer."

A quiet panic resounded inside him. "Is your finger swollen? Are you allergic to it? If you can't wear gold I'll buy you sterling silver." Even as he asked these questions he knew what the answers were.

"No, nothing like that," she replied, her gaze not quite meeting his, but remaining on the ring on the table. "I can't wear it because it's a promise of something that's never going to happen." She finally looked up at him. "I'm not going to marry you, Kyle."

A sharp ache pierced through him, an ache unlike anything he'd ever experienced before. He willed it away and sat down next to her, careful not to touch her. "Joanna, you're tired and not thinking clearly."

Her eyes flashed darkly. "Don't tell me what I'm feeling or what I'm thinking. I've done nothing the past week but think, and I know my decision is the best one for both of us." There was a finality in her voice that chilled him.

"Please tell me how this is the best decision for both of us?" he asked, shoving past the chill and reaching for an edge of anger that felt more familiar and comforting.

"You don't have to worry, I promise I'll allow you unlimited visitation rights to our child," she continued as she stood. "And financially I won't expect anything from you. I can manage things on my own."

"Gosh, that's mighty nice of you," he said with sarcasm. He stood, feeling at a distinct disadvantage with her standing while he sat. "But I don't just want unlimited visitation rights. I want to be a father married to the mother of my child."

"Sometimes fate doesn't offer you exactly what you want," she replied.

"This has nothing to do with fate. It has to do with you and me." He glared at her, wondering what in the hell had happened to change her mind. "Joanna, last night you and I made beautiful love to one another. We fell asleep in each other's arms, listening to one another's heartbeats. What happened between then and now?"

"Nothing happened. I knew before we made love last night that I wasn't going to marry you."

He stared at her in amazement, remembering her passionate response to his touch, the intensity of their kisses, the utter completeness he'd felt and knew she had felt when he'd taken possession of her. "You knew you weren't going to marry me and yet you made love to me, then slept in my arms?"

She eyed him with a touch of boldness. "And

you've never made love to or slept with a woman you had no intentions of marrying?''

Kyle knew his features reflected the guilt that stole through him. Of course he had done that…but that was in his past. "But this isn't about me and other women. This is about you and me. You still haven't told me exactly why you don't want to marry me."

She walked to the front window and for a long moment stared outside. When she turned back to him, there was an unyielding rigidity to the set of her shoulders, and a firm resolution radiating from her eyes.

"You've asked me a hundred times why on the first night we met, I sneaked away from you in the middle of the night. When we finished making love and later I went into the bathroom, I saw your identification and realized you were military. I promised myself a long time ago that I would never, ever become involved with a military man."

"Because of your father." It was a statement rather than a question. She'd spoken enough about her unhappy childhood for him to understand where she was coming from.

"Joanna, we've talked about this," he said with more patience than he felt. "There's no way our baby will have the same experiences you had. You'll be a full-time mother and I'll be an active and interested father when I'm home."

"That's not good enough," she protested.

"Let me guess—you want me to quit the military, stop flying and take a desk job at my father's business. What did you and my father do? Somehow put your heads together to put pressure on me?'' Bitterness rang in Kyle's voice.

''Why are you so angry with your father?''

He drew a deep breath and raked a hand through his hair, thrown by the sudden turn of topic. ''I told you last night that I'm not angry with my father. I get irritated with him for constantly pressuring me to go to work for Ramsey Enterprises, but it's nothing more than that.''

He could tell by the expression on her face that she didn't believe him, and that made his anger rise another notch. ''What on earth does my relationship with my father have to do with you and me?''

She flinched at his sharp tone, but thrust her chin out defiantly. ''I'll tell you what it has to do with us. I need to know if there is unsettled baggage between you and your father that might influence the way you father your own child.''

Kyle stared at her in bewilderment. ''I don't understand the connection between the two.''

The defiance that had momentarily buoyed her seemed to seep away, leaving her appearing more fragile, more tired than before.

Again he swept his hand through his hair in frustration. ''I don't want to fight with you, Joanna,'' he said softly. ''But the reasons you keep giving for not marrying me don't seem like such a big deal.''

Her eyes darkened. ''Okay, then I'll give you the biggest reason of all why I'm not going to marry you.'' She drew a deep breath, as if needing the extra oxygen to sustain her. ''Because we don't love each other.''

His initial reaction to her words was to protest loudly and vehemently, but he couldn't. "We admire and respect each other. We enjoy spending time together. We're great in bed together. Certainly successful marriages have been built on far less."

Her gaze held his intently. "But I've decided I don't want to settle for less. When I get married I want it to be to a man who loves me…a man I love."

Of all the arguments she might have presented, he didn't know how to battle this one. He watched wordlessly as she walked back over to the coffee table and picked up the glittering diamond ring.

"Take it, Kyle," she said, her voice little more than a whisper. "Please take it, because I am not going to wear it anymore."

He knew he should step forward and take it from her, but his feet refused to move. He knew that if he took the ring, it would be an irrevocable act, that once the ring touched his fingers, it would never again be worn on hers.

"I don't want the ring back right now. Look, we went to bed late and got up early. I know you have to be exhausted. Why don't I get out of here and let you take a nap, then I'll come back later this evening and we can talk some more?"

She opened her mouth to protest, but he held up a hand to still her response. "Please, rest now and we'll talk later."

He wanted to kiss her. He wanted to wrap his arms around her and kiss her until she agreed to once again wear his ring, agreed to be his wife. But he knew kissing her would accomplish nothing at the moment.

Instead he looked at her for a long, lingering moment, then turned and left her house. As he got into his car, a dull ache throbbed in his chest.

Tension, he told himself. That's what the pain was—tension and stress. He'd finally managed to embrace the idea of being married to Joanna, of being a father to their baby, and she'd suddenly yanked the rug out from beneath him.

What had happened to change her mind? As recently as the night before she had come to him willingly and eagerly in a bout of lovemaking that had been explosive and mind numbing. He'd seen the tears sparkling on her cheeks as he'd taken her, but he'd thought they were tears of joy, tears produced by the intensity of their joining.

And what was all that nonsense about his father and him? Sure, there was some tension between them, tension because the old man pushed and shoved in an attempt to transform Kyle from an exciting top gun pilot to a three-piece business suit stooge.

He drove aimlessly. He didn't want to go back to the apartment, didn't want to see his father or his brother at the moment. He didn't want to have to explain that the woman he'd introduced as his fiancée the night before wasn't anymore.

As he drove, he tried to arrange his thoughts for when he'd see her again that evening. Hopefully, with a nice, long nap, she'd come to her senses and resume wearing his ring. Hopefully, the current situation was just a touch of craziness induced by overtiredness and hormones.

Still, he was aware that he had no words to counter her final reason why they shouldn't marry. She wanted to marry a man she loved…a man who loved her. Kyle knew he could work hard at making her love him, but he didn't know how to explain to her that loving her wasn't possible. Kyle had decided long ago that loving anyone simply wasn't an option in his life.

He'd loved his father when he'd been younger, but that love had died beneath his father's neglect. Kyle had realized then that loving somebody required too high of an emotional price. Love made people vulnerable, and Kyle never wanted to be vulnerable again. He absolutely refused to consider the possibility of loving Joanna.

For a few minutes after he left, Joanna wandered the confines of the house, playing and replaying their conversation in her head.

Finally, she stretched out on her bed and tried to sleep. She was exhausted. Her eyes were gritty and her head pounded unpleasantly, but still sleep remained elusive.

Her physical tiredness wasn't half as deep or profound as her mental exhaustion. Now that she'd finally come to a decision about the marriage, she should be feeling some sort of relief.

But she didn't.

All she felt was heartache.

She squeezed her eyes tightly shut, attempting to control the tears that threatened. She didn't want to cry. She shouldn't even feel like crying. After all, she'd made the best possible decision for everyone concerned.

But even knowing this, she felt her heartache grow and expand inside her, until she could no longer hold back the tears that burned. They released themselves with a deep sob, and she rolled over on her tummy and wept into her pillow.

She'd given him all kinds of openings, every opportunity she could think of for him to tell her he loved her. But those words had never crossed his lips.

He doesn't love you, her heart cried. He wants to marry you to do the right thing, to be a part of his baby's life, but he doesn't love you. He loves making love to you and the excitement of your sexual relationship, but he doesn't love you.

Joanna had never felt such physical and emotional pain. Invisible hands squeezed her heart and cold claws of pain ripped through her.

She would never, ever fulfill the dreams she'd held on to since childhood. She couldn't imagine ever loving anyone as deeply, as profoundly as she loved Kyle.

She adored his charming smile, the way his eyes lit with humor. She respected his abilities as a pilot and his commitment to his work. She liked the way he made her laugh, the way he made her feel so pretty, so desirable, so…special.

A sob caught in her throat. She even liked the way he tied his shoes and buttered his bread. The only thing she didn't love about him was the fact that he didn't love her.

Finally, mercifully, she fell asleep.

It was nearly three hours later when she awakened, feeling physically refreshed and emotionally stronger. She got out of bed and took a long, hot shower, then fixed herself a sandwich and sat down at the table to write a note to Kyle.

There was no way she was going to let him in here for another go-around. She was neither mentally nor physically strong enough to continue arguing with him.

She'd made up her mind, she'd given him plenty of reasons why she didn't intend to marry him, and now she was through discussing or arguing about it.

After writing the note, she sealed it in an envelope, then taped it to the outside of her front door. She had no idea what time he might return, but she didn't intend to open up when he did.

Her car was parked in the windowless garage and she carefully pulled the shades over all the windows, so he wouldn't know if she were home or not.

Truth be told, she was afraid to talk to him anymore, afraid that her resolve wasn't as strong as it should be.

She was afraid that he'd look at her with those gorgeous gray eyes of his, that he might touch her ever so gently, and she would crumble and give in to whatever he wanted.

And she knew saying yes to Kyle's marriage proposal was the same as saying yes to a lifetime of heartbreak.

It was almost seven when she heard his knock on her front door. She'd been sitting on the sofa reading a book, without the television on, with no radio playing, wanting the silence of the interior to tell him she wasn't in.

Stealthily she rose from the sofa and went to the front door. She placed her palms on it, as if she might feel his essence radiating through the thick wood.

"Joanna," he called softly. "I know you're in there. Open up, let me come in."

Not by the hair of my chinny chin chin. She bit her lip to stifle a hysterical giggle as the old fairy tale came to mind.

"Please, Joanna. Open the door so we can talk."

Her fingers itched to move to the lock, to throw the bolt and allow him entry. But she fought the impulse, knowing absolutely nothing good could come of it.

It was over. Finished. Her mind was made up. And he was just going to have to accept this.

"Joanna, I'm not going to let this go," he said, as if he'd read her mind through the door. "We can build a good life together."

She closed her eyes, fighting the evocative pull of his words. Damn him. Damn him for making this so difficult. Damn him for his deep voice that sent rivulets of heat through her, that made tears once again burn in her eyes.

She'd thought she was all cried out, but where he was concerned there seemed to be an endless supply of tears. She wiped her cheeks angrily. He was only being persistent because of the baby.

"Joanna, for God's sake, let me in and let's talk."

There was a long moment of silence, then he said

her name a final time and she heard the sound of his footsteps fading as he walked back down the sidewalk. A moment later she heard the engine of his car roar to life.

She slumped against the door. And so it was done. He was out of her life. Now, if she could just figure out a way to get him out of her head and out of her heart...

But it wasn't done, she discovered the next morning. When she left her house to go to the base, she was shocked to see his car pulled up at the curb in front of her place.

He got out of the car and hurried toward her, reaching the garage door before she could. "I told you in my note yesterday that I thought it was better if we drove to work separately," she said, and reached for the garage door handle.

He beat her to it and pulled up the door. "And I told you I don't think it's a good idea for you to come and go all alone in your condition."

"Kyle, I'm pregnant, not terminally ill," she said impatiently. She was angry that he was here. She was angry that even though she'd made her choice, despite the fact that it was done and over as far as she was concerned, his handsome presence made her heart beat faster, caused a curl of desire to unfurl in the pit of her stomach.

"I'd just feel better if I follow you to and from work every day," he said.

"Suit yourself." She walked past him and got into her car. She had to stay strong, and the way to stay strong was to have as little contact with him as possible.

She backed out of the garage and he closed the door. Without giving him time to return to his car, she pulled away.

It took only minutes of driving for her to look in her rearview mirror and see him directly behind her. Why couldn't he just leave it alone? Leave *her* alone?

How long would this mission go on? How many days, weeks, months would she have to work with Kyle? How many days and nights would she have to see him—love him—and reject him? Was she strong enough to see him day in and day out and continue to rebuff his advances?

Maybe it was time to put in her resignation. She knew that eventually she'd have to do it. She had enough money saved to be able to live comfortably, yet frugally, without working for about a year. And she knew when the baby was born she wasn't going to work...not for a long while.

Yes, perhaps it was time to give herself and Ambassador Templeton a firm date of resignation. If she gave a month's notice, she would know she only had thirty more days to see Kyle.

She sighed wearily and shot a glance in her rearview mirror. At the moment thirty days seemed like an eternity.

Chapter 13

It was after midnight when Kyle crept into his family apartment. He went from the foyer directly into the kitchen and grabbed a soft drink from the refrigerator.

Leaning against the cabinets, he popped the top and took a deep drink, fighting the depression that had threatened to overwhelm him for the past three days.

It had been three days since Joanna had taken off his engagement ring and placed it on the coffee table before him. And for the past three days Kyle had tried everything in his power to try to change her mind.

He'd sent her flowers and a box of silk scarves, but each delivery had been rejected. He parked in front of her house each morning and followed her home each night when their shift was over, hoping to get an opportunity to talk to her, to reason with her, but she refused to even speak to him.

The only time she'd said anything substantial to him had been this afternoon, when she'd mentioned that she had a meeting with Ambassador Templeton tomorrow morning, and that there was no reason for Kyle to hang out in front of her house.

Funny, he had spent his entire life avoiding the ties of marriage, and now when he wanted to marry Joanna, she was the master at avoidance.

Why was she letting the crazy concept of love interfere with their plans? Why couldn't she see that the basis they had for marriage was much stronger than the mere fantasy of love?

He finished his soft drink, dropped the can in the trash and then started through the living room toward his bedroom.

"Kyle."

He jumped in surprise at the sound of his father's voice. "Jeez, Major," he exclaimed as he turned on the light and found his father sitting in a chair. "What are you doing here in the dark in the middle of the night?"

"Waiting for you. I'd like to talk to you, Kyle."

Dread rolled through him. "I'm tired. Can't it wait until morning?" he asked.

Edward shook his head. "Tyler and I are flying out first thing in the morning. I really need to talk to you, Son. Please."

Kyle knew that he'd spent the days his father and brother had been here avoiding this very conversation, but looking at his father, he couldn't deny Edward the opportunity to speak with him now.

"Okay," he said, and sat in the wing chair opposite. "So, give me the spiel," he said, assuming their conversation would follow the pattern of many they'd had before.

"Before I begin my *spiel,* I want to know what's going on with you."

Kyle frowned at his father. "What do you mean?"

Edward held his gaze for a long moment. "You're unhappy and it's obvious. I feel your unhappiness deep inside my heart."

Kyle eyed his father in surprise. "You're shocked," Edward continued dryly. "Kyle, don't you realize that your unhappiness becomes mine because I love you?"

It was the same kind of thing King Marcus had said when he'd spoken of his wife's tears scalding his cheeks, her heartache being felt in his chest.

Love. Kyle couldn't remember the last time his father had told him he loved him, and the words somehow seeped into his skin, into his very soul, and found dark places he hadn't known existed.

But along with the warmth caused by his father's words came a surge of disbelief, then anger.

"Yeah, right, you love me despite the fact I'm a huge disappointment to you." Kyle felt a swell of emotion inside him, a frightening emotion that had tormented him in the deepest dark of night for as long as he could remember.

This time it was Edward's turn to look shocked.

"My God, Kyle, whatever gave you the idea that you are a disappointment to me?"

Pressure expanded in Kyle's chest, a suffocating pressure that for just a moment made speech impossible. He stood and paced in front of his father, trying to gather his thoughts before speaking again.

He stalked the confines of the room, then threw himself back into the chair across from his father. "I've never understood why you've tried so hard to get me out of the military. Is it because you think I'm not good enough to carry on the tradition of excellence that you set?"

"Is that what you really believe?" Edward shook his head, suddenly looking older than his sixty-four years. "Oh, Son, we should have had this talk a long time ago."

Kyle watched as his father rose and walked over to the bar and poured himself a snifter of brandy, then returned to his chair. "Kyle, I've tried to stop you from following in my footsteps because I don't want to see you make the same mistakes that I did."

Kyle frowned, confused. "What kind of mistakes? You were a decorated war hero."

"I was a young soldier, thrown into a battle I didn't understand, who happened to do the right things at the right time."

Edward leaned back in the chair and took a sip of the brandy, obviously gathering his thoughts. Kyle waited patiently, the ball of emotion still tight in his chest.

"I remember the exact moment I realized what I'd done...just what I had lost," Edward said, his voice low and his tone reflective. "You were fourteen years old and I was home on leave and we were all sitting at the kitchen table having breakfast."

Kyle frowned at his father, unsure what a foray into the distant past had to do with anything. Was his father getting to the age where his mind wandered?

Edward gazed down into his brandy, as if seeing a movie of memories unfolding in the liquid. "I remember the sun coming in the kitchen window and striking you on the side of your face, and I saw that you had whiskers." Edward looked at Kyle, his expression one of shock. "Whiskers," he repeated.

"Dad," Kyle said with a touch of impatience. "I have no idea what you're talking about."

"I'm talking about time and priorities." Edward took another sip of his brandy, his gaze intent on his son. "Until that moment in the kitchen, I thought I had plenty of time to be around while you were growing up. And then I saw those whiskers on your cheeks and realized my little boy was already almost a man, and I'd missed all those important years with him."

"But you were doing something important, and I understood that," Kyle said. The tightness in his chest increased, constricting like bands of steel around his heart. "You were a hero. There wasn't a day of my childhood that I didn't brag about you."

"And there wasn't a day that went by that you weren't just a little bit angry that I wasn't home where I belonged," Edward countered. "And through the years that anger has grown. We should have addressed it with one another a long time ago."

"That's ridiculous," Kyle scoffed. "I was never angry with you." Yet even as he spoke the words, the emotion inside him exploded, and to his horror he felt the sting of tears in his eyes.

He stood and walked to the window again, hurriedly turning away from his father, appalled by his weakness, appalled by the need he felt.

"I knew you were doing something important," Kyle repeated, his voice faint…unsteady. "You were a hero."

"Stop saying that." Edward's voice rang out sharply, and Kyle turned back to face him in surprise. Edward set his glass down on the floor beside his chair, then stood and approached Kyle.

"I was no hero, Son. I was just a man—a man who made choices that took me away from my family. I missed first steps, first words, your first Little League game—all those precious moments that I can never get back. I saw the world from the cockpit of an airplane, but I didn't see my firstborn son growing up."

"But even after you quit the military, you were still gone, building your empire," Kyle replied, and heard the bitterness in his own voice.

"That's not true," Edward countered. "When I quit the military, I was home, but you weren't. Kyle, you were a young teenager. You had your own friends and activities. I was around, but you weren't."

Edward placed his hands on Kyle's shoulders. "I

love you, Kyle, and I don't want to see you sacrifice home and family and love for flying a plane. I don't want you to make my mistakes and waste precious time.''

Kyle had never before realized just how hungry he'd been all of his life for his father's love, but now, seeing it shine from Edward's eyes, feeling it wash over him in warm waves, he felt something break inside of him.

It was at that moment that Kyle recognized he *had* been angry with his father, an anger that had festered for years. He'd built his father into a hero bigger than life in order to cope with a little boy's feelings of abandonment.

Then he realized something else—it hadn't been anger, it had been hurt, a hurt that had transformed into anger because anger was something Kyle understood, something that felt familiar.

But now, seeing the remorse, the pain of those lost years reflected in his father's eyes, he felt a fragile healing begin. Tears blurred Kyle's vision and a sob burst from his throat.

His father pulled him into a bear hug and Kyle gripped him as he'd wanted to for all those years.

They held on to one another for a very long time, and as he hugged his father, Kyle felt the anger he'd suppressed for so long fall away and the hurt he'd harbored deep inside dissipate. A peace he'd never known before seeped through him and his heart opened in a way it never had before.

And in his heart came a new pain—the pain of realizing he might never be Joanna's husband, might never get the opportunity to truly father his own child.

Kyle released his dad and stepped back from him. "Joanna broke off our engagement. She's having my baby and I want to marry her, but she refuses." The words tumbled from him, one right after the other. "I don't know how to make her listen to reason." He looked at his father helplessly.

Edward reached out and patted Kyle's shoulder, then sat back down in his chair. "Has she told you why she doesn't want to marry you?"

"She's given me several reasons." Kyle slumped back in the chair across from his father. He felt unreasonably vulnerable. Although he knew that the rift that had existed between them had begun a beautiful healing process, that didn't explain the weight that still pulled at his heart.

"Joanna had a terrible childhood. Her mother died when she was born and her father was military and gone all the time," Kyle explained. "She was raised by housekeepers and nannies, some who weren't very nice to her." Kyle thought of the story she'd told him about her invisible sister, and his heart constricted with sadness for her.

"Anyway, she told me she doesn't want to live a military lifestyle, she doesn't want to raise her child on a series of bases with a husband who is gone most of the time."

Edward remained silent, but Kyle knew what he was thinking. He was hoping Kyle wouldn't follow in his footsteps and try to juggle a family with covert and dangerous missions.

Kyle rubbed the center of his forehead, where a headache had begun to pound. He didn't tell his father the other reason why Joanna didn't intend to marry him—that apparently she didn't love him.

"I don't know what to do, Dad," he confessed. "I think maybe if I give up the military then I could convince her to marry me, but I can't imagine a life without flying planes."

Edward leaned forward. "Perhaps I can help by offering a compromise of sorts."

"A compromise?"

Edward bent down and picked up his glass of brandy. "When I came here to speak with you about your plans for reenlistment, I never intended to offer you a position at Ramsey Enterprises."

"You didn't?" Kyle stared at the man who was suddenly full of surprises.

"I have a different kind of job offer for you, but first you must promise me you'll never repeat what I'm about to tell you."

"Okay." Kyle leaned forward in turn, intrigued by the glint of secrets in his father's eyes.

Edward tipped his glass and finished the last of his brandy, then settled back in the chair, his gaze once again distant and reflective.

"It began a long time ago...during the Vietnam War. I met up with some men who were like me— decorated war heroes trying to make sense of the world. That was certainly not the war to try to make sense of," he said with a wry shake of his head. "After the war and through the years, we kept in touch, and we spoke often of our disillusionment with how bureaucracy got in the way of freedom.''

A chill began inside Kyle as he recognized Ambassador Templeton saying the same kind of thing when he'd been telling Kyle about the mysterious Noble Men.

"Over the years, the five of us met often, and we worked to achieve personal wealth and affluence so we could eventually achieve our common purpose...world peace.''

"The Noble Men." Kyle's voice was a mere whisper as he tried to take in the enormity of what his father was confessing to him.

Edward smiled. "That's the name others have given us. We're just five men trying to do right in a world that sometimes is all wrong.''

"You said five men. Who—who are the others?" Kyle asked, struggling to take it all in.

"I'm not at liberty to divulge that right now," Edward replied.

Kyle shook his head and stared at his father. Edward Ramsey was one of the Noble Men. Kyle's father was one of the powerful, altruistic leaders working outside the boundaries for world peace. Pride swelled in Kyle's heart at the stunning realization.

His dad worked to promote freedom, to provide safety for women and children and to help unite nations in peace. And he did it anonymously, with no need for medals or rewards.

Shame coursed through Kyle as he thought of all the times he'd thought his father had sold out, had traded honor for the almighty buck. "Dad—"

Edward held up a hand, as if he knew what thoughts were whirling around in his son's head. "No need, Son," he said softly. "There was a time when the five of us did most of our own fieldwork, but time marches on and none of us are young anymore."

"It was you who brought me here on this mission," Kyle said, still stunned by everything he was hearing.

"You are one of the best, Kyle, and we needed one of the best. And we need one of the best now. The Noble Men want to offer you a job training and overseeing the pilots in our employment. There would be almost no traveling, and the work would be mostly regular hours, giving you an opportunity to enjoy other areas of life."

Kyle opened his mouth to speak, but Edward stopped him by raising his hand. "You don't have to give me an answer right now. Just think about it. I know I've thrown a lot at you." He smiled warmly. "It's been a night of illumination on several levels."

Edward stifled a yawn with the back of his hand and stood. "I'm an old man and it's past my bedtime."

Kyle also stood. "What time is your flight in the morning?"

"We need to be at the airport by eight-thirty."

"I'd like to drive you there."

His father's gray eyes held nothing but love. "I'd like that," he said simply.

For the second time that night the two men embraced. "Think about our offer, Kyle," Edward said as he released him. "Perhaps it's the answer to your problem with Joanna. She's a lovely young woman. And I promise you won't regret building your life around having time with her and your child."

Kyle nodded, then watched as his father disappeared down the hallway and into the master suite. Kyle knew he should go to bed, but his head was spinning from the late night events.

His dad was one of the Noble Men, and he loved Kyle and regretted the lost years! Kyle walked over to the windows and stared out into the darkness of the night. With an objectivity he'd never had before, he thought back over his childhood.

He'd needed to see Edward as a hero in order to assuage the heartache of a little boy who missed his father desperately.

Edward had been right. When he'd finally quit the military and had time to spend with his family, Kyle was old enough that he didn't want to spend time with his father. He'd had his own interests to pursue, girls to chase and guy friends to hang out with.

But he'd harbored a wealth of pain because he'd believed his father didn't love him…and he'd spent all of his adult years making sure he never loved and left himself vulnerable again.

Joanna. Her name exploded in his head and shot overwhelming emotion into his heart.

He loved her.

He stumbled from the window to the chair and sank down, stunned by the realization that love for her coursed through his entire body. He'd believed his feelings for her were physical, that he loved making love to her and nothing more. But he'd been lying to himself.

When she laughed, he felt her laughter deep inside him, and when she'd spoken of her make-believe sister's tragic end, her pain had flowed through him.

He didn't want to marry her to do the right thing. He wanted to marry her because he loved her, because she was his heart, his soul, and he couldn't bear to think of living without her.

He looked at the telephone, wanting...*needing* to talk to her now, this moment, when his realization of how he felt was new and fresh and flooding through him. But it was after one in the morning, and she would be sleeping.

Leaning his head back, he closed his eyes and remembered the last time he'd fallen asleep with her in his arms. He should have known what was in his heart then, when her body had been warm against his and he'd been filled with an aching tenderness, a fierce protectiveness.

He pulled himself up and headed for his bedroom. He would wait until morning to talk to Joanna. He'd take his father and brother to the airport, then catch her at the embassy.

Once he was in bed, he stared up at the dark ceiling overhead as a sudden burst of anxiety ripped through him. His military career was only one of the reasons she had given for not wanting to marry him.

I don't want to settle for less. When I get married I want it to be to a man who loves me...a man I love.... The words she'd spoken to him on the day she'd tried to give him back his ring went around

and around in his head. The result was a flurry of
fear that tied a knot in his stomach.

What if him loving her wasn't enough?

He squeezed his eyes tightly shut, refusing to even
contemplate that particular heartbreak. Somehow,
someway, he had to convince her that they belonged
together, that he could love her enough to make up
for the fact that she apparently didn't love him.

Chapter 14

"I am both saddened and joyous at the same time," Nigel Templeton said after Joanna had explained her decision and submitted her resignation effective in two weeks time.

"I am sorry that we are losing your expertise and your dedication." Nigel smiled. "But I'm certainly not going to argue against the importance of motherhood."

Relief flooded through Joanna. This had been the most difficult decision she'd ever made, the decision to give her notice now instead of further into the pregnancy.

But after the last three days—since she'd told Kyle she was not going to marry him—she knew she couldn't handle seeing him every day, loving him every day and knowing there was no future with him.

The last few days had been torture, every moment filled with the heartbreak of unfulfilled dreams and love unrequited.

Thankfully, the ambassador had asked no personal questions about the fact that she was pregnant and not married, and she certainly didn't intend to tell him that Kyle was the father. If Kyle wanted anyone to know he could tell them himself.

"It isn't a decision I've made lightly," she explained. "And I'm sorry for bailing out on you in the middle of the special project." That's how they spoke of the unofficial air patrols over Montebello.

"No need to be sorry. I'll assign Todd Chamberlain to start working with you immediately on the special project, and he will take over your duties when you leave us. I'm assuming that in the next two weeks you can bring him up to snuff."

"No problem," Joanna replied. Todd Chamberlain was bright and ambitious. He would be thrilled at the opportunity to step into her shoes.

"Have you told Lieutenant Commander Ramsey of your decision?"

"No. I'll speak with him this afternoon and let him know." She hoped none of the emotion that rolled inside her at the thought of that particular conversation was evident in her voice.

Ambassador Templeton leaned back in his chair, his gaze warm and his smile friendly. "Do you know what your plans are?"

Joanna returned his smile and shook her head ruefully. "Not really," she admitted. "I'm thinking of returning to the States. I have a little bit of money put away, and with the sale of the house here I should have enough to tide me over for a while."

"I will write you a job recommendation that will gain you whatever position in whatever field you desire," Nigel said.

Warmth for the man she'd worked for flooded through her, along with the threat of tears, but the tears didn't materialize and she knew why. She'd lost all the moisture from her body crying over Kyle.

"I appreciate all that you've taught me while I've worked here. Working for you has been an experience I'll never forget," she said.

Nigel glanced at his watch, stood and walked around the desk, motioning Joanna to stand as well. "It's easy to teach an intelligent and willing student. And now, much as I hate it, I have another appointment to get to. Come, walk out with me."

They left his inner office and stepped into the reception area. Nigel took her hands in his and began to speak—but his words were lost as a tremendous explosion thundered around them.

The powerful blast shattered windows and crumbled walls. Shards of glass flew like tiny missiles, and dust and smoke billowed.

It was an explosion not only of sound, but of displaced air as well. The force ripped the ambassador's hands from hers, and Joanna was thrown backward.

She sailed through the air and slammed into the wall behind her. With a confused groan, she fell to the floor. The sound of screams was the last thing she heard before darkness descended and she knew no more.

* * *

Kyle gave his brother a hug, then clapped him on the back. "Take care, Tyler, and don't give Dad too hard a time," he said, then turned to his father.

Edward pulled his eldest son into a heartfelt bear hug, and again Kyle felt love surge inside him. "Dad," he said as they parted. "I'm so glad we talked."

"Me, too," Edward agreed. "I'm only sorry it took us so long. We've wasted a lot of time."

Kyle nodded. "But things will be different in the future. I'll call you about the other topic we talked about," he added, referring to his father's job offer.

Edward nodded and they all said their final goodbyes. Minutes later Kyle left the terminal and headed for his car in the parking lot.

He felt better than he had in years. The healing that had taken place between his father and himself had opened Kyle's heart to all kinds of emotions he'd never allowed himself before.

He regretted the years he had carried a grudge against his father, meeting him with cold defensiveness instead of with the love he'd always harbored for the man.

Regret ran deep for the years they had lost—years wasted because of pride and because of stubbornness. They couldn't reclaim the time they had missed, but hopefully his father had lots of years left for Kyle to enjoy.

Thoughts of his father fell away as nervous energy filled his veins. Joanna. Her name sang in his heart and rang in his brain.

The moment his eyes had opened that morning,

he'd wanted to call Joanna and shower her with his love, but he'd decided that what he wanted to tell her was too important to do in an impersonal phone call.

Hopefully, he would catch her as she left the embassy. He wanted to take her in his arms, pull her against his pounding heart and confess all the love for her that burned inside him. He could only pray that it would be enough for her to take a chance on him, to agree to bind her life with his.

He hadn't given his father an answer about the training position simply because it depended on how his conversation with Joanna went. If she agreed to marry him, then there was nothing he'd like more than to have a job that brought him home to her every night.

But if she continued to refuse to marry him, then he wasn't sure he could take the job without his heart breaking in two.

He looked at his watch. It was just a few minutes after nine. Joanna had said her appointment with the ambassador was for nine o'clock. Kyle had plenty of time to get to the embassy and wait for her. Leaning forward, he turned on the radio, hoping a little music would soothe his nerves.

"...Repeating our breaking news, there has been an explosion at the American Embassy in Montebello. Unidentified sources indicate that the blast was a bomb."

A rush of noise filled Kyle's ears and it took him a moment to realize it was the sound of surging blood as his heart pounded with frantic intensity.

No! Surely he hadn't heard right. As the station he was listening to immediately began playing an oldie tune, Kyle swerved his car to the curb and furiously punched the radio buttons, seeking any station that might be broadcasting news.

"...American Embassy, and preliminary reports suggest that it was a bomb. Officials are requesting that everyone stay out of the area, as emergency vehicles and personnel are on the scene."

Kyle felt as if his heart was exploding in his chest. Joanna! His brain screamed her name over and over again as he screeched away from the curb, unmindful of the traffic he cut off with his frantic maneuver.

He had to get to the embassy. Dear God, he had to get to Joanna. He shut off the radio, afraid of what he might hear. He was surprised by the noise that continued despite the abrupt silence of the radio. It took him a moment to realize the sound was him praying for Joanna's safety. It was the sound of him sobbing, afraid that he wouldn't have a chance to have a future with her and their child, afraid that he would never be able to tell her how much he loved her.

It took him ten minutes to get within three blocks of the embassy. There, he found the streets barricaded by police officers.

He parked and continued on foot, eluding the guards as he raced toward the rising smoke that blackened the sky above. His team had guarded the skies against attack, alert for any kind of an air strike. But it was impossible to guard against attacks when the enemy got up close and personal with an indiscriminate bomb.

As the embassy came into view, his heart knocked even harder against his ribs. Shattered glass was everywhere and smoke swirled from the roof. There was a gaping hole where the windows on the fifth floor had once been...the windows of Ambassador Templeton's office.

For just a moment Kyle's legs threatened to buckle and he thought he might fall to his knees. "Joanna," he whispered, and hurried forward, afraid of what he would find.

Ambulances and emergency equipment clogged the street in front of the building. As Kyle approached, two of the ambulances pulled away, their sirens screaming of life-and-death drama.

Kyle hurried toward the front of the building but was stopped by a security guard. "Sir, I must ask you to leave the area."

Kyle fumbled for his identification. "I'm Lieutenant Commander Ramsey."

"I don't care if you're a visiting king, we are trying to make sure everyone is out of there, and only rescue units are allowed in."

"But you don't understand," Kyle exclaimed, fighting the impulse to physically move the guard aside and rush past him. "My fiancée works in there. I've got to get inside."

The guard's gaze softened. "I'm sorry, Lieutenant Commander, but I really can't let you pass. Everyone who worked in there was a husband or a wife, a mother or a father, a brother or a sister. Besides, the last report I heard was that they believe the building has been successfully evacuated.''

"Were there fatalities?" The words tore from Kyle throat.

"I don't know," the guard replied softly. "Nobody is releasing that kind of information yet. But I can tell you this—all the injured have been taken either to Montebello General Hospital or to the military hospital on the base."

"Thanks," Kyle said as he whirled around and raced back to his car. He was aware of seconds... minutes ticking by, precious moments during which Joanna might be fighting for, clinging to life.

His urgency to find her, to get to her, was all-consuming. Panic surged inside him, squeezing his gut, constricting his heart. She had to be all right. Dear God, please let her be all right.

The Montebello General Hospital emergency room was packed with people. Weeping women and cursing men with cuts and contusions filled every chair and stood in groups, apparently waiting their turn for medical attention.

Kyle scanned the faces frantically, seeking the one he was most desperate to see. But Joanna wasn't in there. He raced to the desk, where a harassed nurse held a phone receiver in one hand and was clicking on a computer mouse with the other.

"Joanna Morgan? Has she been admitted?" Kyle asked.

The nurse frowned and shook her head, indicating that he should wait for her to get off the phone. "I'm sorry, we can't give out that kind of information," she said into the phone. "You will have to contact one of the hospital administrators for an official statement."

She slammed down the receiver. "You'd think the press would know better than to call an emergency room in the middle of a crisis. Now, what was that name?"

"Morgan. Joanna Morgan," Kyle said.

His heart raced anxiously as he watched the nurse type the name into the computer. She shook her head. "We don't have anyone by that name back in the ER or recently admitted." Her blue eyes were soft with sympathy. "She was at the embassy?" Kyle nodded. "Then perhaps she was taken to the base hospital."

Before the words were completely out of her mouth, Kyle turned and hurried out of the hospital. He felt sick to his stomach as he got into his car and headed toward the military base.

He had faced enemy fighter pilots, had participated in life-and-death air battles, had made emergency landings under extremely poor conditions, but nothing he'd ever experienced sent such panic, such utter fear through him as what he felt now.

The thought of life without Joanna filled him with a hopeless despair. Surely fate wouldn't be so cruel as to open up his heart to love, then snatch away the opportunity of any future.

And yet he knew the perverse nature of fate, knew that people died, lives were shattered and hearts were broken every day.

If she wasn't at the base hospital, there was only

two other places she could be—trapped beneath rubble at the embassy, or lying on a slab in a morgue.

A sob rose up inside him, ripping from his throat
along with a hoarse curse. Damn the people responsible for this! Damn the people who fought with
bombs and killed or maimed the innocent.

Agonizing minutes later, Kyle rushed into the base
hospital emergency room. Like the other one, it too
was filled with people—bomb victims waiting to see
a doctor and people waiting for loved ones. A crowd
stood around the desk, making it impossible for Kyle
to even see the nurse working there.

Again he looked for Joanna among the wounded,
but she was nowhere to be found. He didn't even
attempt to get to the nurse at the desk, but instead
barreled through the double doors that led to the
emergency room cubicles.

"Sir!" a nurse called after him as he flew to the
first examining room and threw back the curtain. An
elderly man sat on the bed, his arm at an unnatural
angle.

"Sir, stop!" The nurse's voice was brisk and more
than a little bit irritated as Kyle went to the next
examining room. Before he could pull open the next
curtain, she grabbed him by the arm.

"I have to find her." Kyle spun around to face
the nurse, and the control he'd fought so hard to
maintain from the moment he'd heard the first news-
cast slipped away.

He grabbed the nurse by the shoulders. "She's got
to be in here. She's got to be. Don't you understand,
I've looked everywhere, and if she isn't here—" He

broke off, another sob welling up inside him and bringing with it a dark abyss of pain too intense to endure.

"Kyle?"

The achingly familiar voice pierced through him and he released his hold on the startled nurse as Joanna stepped out of a nearby examining room.

"Joanna. Thank God," he whispered, then rushed forward and wrapped his arms around her, blinking back tears of relief.

Joanna held herself stiff for only a minute, then melted against him, needing to be held after the horror of what she'd just endured.

For a very long moment she remained unmoving, held so close to him she could feel the frantic pounding of his heart. She'd been shocked when she'd heard his voice, then realized that of course he'd be worried…worried about the baby she carried.

She pulled away from him, shocked to see his eyes glistening with what appeared to be tears. Tears? Kyle Ramsey was crying?

"Are you all right?" he asked as she stepped out of his embrace.

"The baby is fine, Kyle," she replied, assuming that's what he wanted, needed to hear.

"That's good…but are *you* all right?" He placed his palms on either side of her face, his gray eyes holding a wildness, an edge of panic she'd never seen before.

"The doctor just assured me I'm fine. I'm bruised,

and I have a lump on my head where something hit me, but other than that, I'm okay.''

"I'm sorry, but I must ask that the two of you take your conversation somewhere else," the nurse exclaimed. "We have a waiting room full of people to attend to."

Kyle took Joanna's hand and started to pull her back toward the examining room she'd just exited. "No, Kyle. The doctor released me. I'm free to go."

"Are you sure you're all right?" he asked, the wildness still in his eyes.

"I'm fine, really. I just want to go home."

She didn't fight him when he placed an arm around her shoulder. Instead, she leaned slightly into him, wanting…needing his strength.

Now that the initial burst of adrenaline and fear had passed, she felt cold and slightly sick to her stomach. She felt as if she'd just survived the worst kind of nightmare imaginable, and at least for this moment, she was grateful to have Kyle to hang on to. She didn't want to be alone.

He opened the passenger car door for her, then fastened the seat belt around her. The simple gesture felt oddly intimate, and she leaned her head back and closed her eyes, steeling herself against his closeness.

Moments later, he slid behind the wheel and started the engine. "Want to talk about it?" he asked softly.

"No…yes." She opened her eyes and sat up. And to her surprise, she burst into tears. She buried her face in her hands, weeping weakly, knowing her tears were a delayed reaction.

Kyle pulled the car over to the side of the road, unbuckled his seat belt and got out. She was vaguely aware of him coming to her side of the car and opening her door. There, he unbuckled her own seat belt, then pulled her into his arms.

"Shh," he whispered as she sobbed into his chest. "You're safe now." He stroked her hair with such tenderness it only made her cry harder.

She cried from fear, remembering that moment when she'd come to after the blast and realized what had happened. The horror of the scene sent chills up and down her spine. And she cried because in Kyle's arms she found a comforting safety that she knew would never be hers again.

Finally, she drew a ragged breath, tears spent. "It was so awful," she said, not moving from his arms. "One minute I was saying goodbye to the ambassador, and the next minute I was picking myself up across the room." She shivered and Kyle tightened his grip on her. "Thank God we left his office when we did, because I think the bomb was in there."

"Let's get you home where you belong," Kyle said. She nodded and he left her side. She rebuckled her seat belt, leaned back and once again closed her eyes.

"Could you turn on the news?" she asked once the car was again in motion.

"Are you sure?"

She nodded without opening her eyes. "Positive. I want to hear what's happening."

"...Our top story is that a bomb has rocked the American Embassy. Preliminary reports indicate that there have been no fatalities. I repeat, no fatalities have been reported.''

''Thank God,'' Kyle murmured.

Joanna released a sigh of relief. ''You can turn it off now,'' she said. ''That's what I wanted to hear.''

Neither of them said another word until the car came to a stop and Joanna finally opened her eyes. One glance out the window told her Kyle had not driven to her house, but rather to the Ramsey apartment.

''I thought you were taking me home,'' she protested weakly, too tired to fight. She was suddenly more exhausted than she'd ever been in her life.

''I just spent agonizing minutes afraid I had lost you. I'm not ready to let you out of my sight.''

There was something odd in his voice, but she was too tired to figure out exactly what it was. She allowed him to help her out of the car and up to his apartment.

When they got inside the front door, he scooped her up in his arms and carried her toward his bedroom. There, he placed her gently on the bed, then covered her with a lightweight blanket. ''You rest,'' he said, then he kissed her on the forehead and left the room.

Within minutes, Joanna was asleep.

She awakened with the golden light of dusk painting the room, and was surprised to see Kyle lying next to her, gazing at her with an intensity that stirred something deep inside her.

She knew she should sit up, escape the magic that

resided in the sweet gray depths of his eyes. She stirred, but he placed a hand on the side of her face.

"I love you, Joanna."

She must still be sleeping, she reasoned to herself. She was still asleep and dreaming the sweetest dream in the world. But if she were dreaming would his hand feel so warm, so achingly tender against her cheek?

Frowning, she returned his stare. "Am I awake?"

He laughed. "I certainly hope so, because I've waited just about as long as I possibly can to tell you how much I love you and how much I want to spend the rest of my life with you."

Joanna sat up, emotion welling inside her. She knew it was nothing more than the craziness of the day that had prompted his words...that, or it was simply manipulation to get her to agree to marry him.

"Don't, Kyle." She pushed her hair away from her face, trying to focus on something besides his nearness and the words he had just spoken. "I...I need to get home. I need to make some calls, listen to the reports and find out what's going on."

He sat up as well, a deep frown worrying the center of his forehead. "I've done nothing but make calls, take calls and listen to reports all afternoon. I can tell you whatever you want to know.

"The bomb was small, and thankfully, most of the force of it went outward, toward the street, instead of inward into the building. There was no structural damage, although a lot of cosmetic wreckage. Everyone who was in the building has been accounted for, and the injuries consist mostly of broken bones and cuts and abrasions.''

"No fatalities?''

He shook his head. "None. They've made an arrest.''

"Really?''

"He's been identified as Muhammad Oman, and he's saying he was hired by Kamal to set the bomb. Kamal has already issued an official denial.''

"So who is this Muhammad Oman?'' she asked.

"News sources are reporting that he's a hired gun used by many international terrorist organizations, but so far nobody has managed to officially connect him to Kamal. However, the embassy wasn't the only place there was unusual activity.''

"What do you mean?''

"While everyone was sorting out the bombing at the embassy, a kidnapping attempt was made on Princess Julia. Thankfully, the attempt failed, but the men who tried to grab her got away.''

"Is Sheik Ahmed Kamal responsible?'' Joanna asked.

"Nobody knows, but that's what King Marcus believes. Everyone in his family must now be kept under closer guard, especially now that Princess Julia has broken down in the wake of the kidnapping and admitted that the child she carries is indeed Rashid Kamal's. The King is not only tightening security around the royal palace, but he's also sending a guy named Jack Dalton to the United States to act as bodyguard to Princess Christina, who is working in the U.S. as a research scientist.''

"Who is Jack Dalton?" she asked, her head reeling.

"The son of a friend of my father's. He's a former Navy SEAL. Didn't you hear what I said earlier?" Kyle blurted out in obvious frustration.

"I heard." She swung her legs over the edge of the bed and stood. "But the bombing has made everything a little crazy."

He got up and approached where she stood. "I'm not a little crazy. I'm a lot crazy in love with you, and I knew I was before the bomb exploded."

He was mere inches in front of her, and she tried not to notice the familiar scent of him, the evocative heat that flowed from his body.

"I'm not reenlisting. I found out last night that my father helped fund our mission here. He's part of a group called the Noble Men."

"The Noble Men?"

He nodded. "I'll explain it all to you later. What I need to tell you now is that I'm finished with my military career. My father and the Noble Men have offered me a position as a flight instructor in the States, training and overseeing the pilots they employ. I'm taking the job."

Her gaze flew to his in surprise. "But I don't want you to do that for me," she protested. Damn. Damn. Why was everything so difficult where he was concerned?

"I'm not doing it for you. I'm doing it for me." He placed his hands on her shoulders, as if wanting to assure himself she couldn't get away, couldn't escape before he said what he had to say. "I want a job that will see me home every night...home with the woman I love. I want a house where we'll live for years, building memories and raising children.''

Joanna stared at him, wanting desperately to fall into the beautiful dream his words painted, but afraid…so afraid to believe him, to believe in the possibility.

''Joanna…I love you, and you were right. I had some baggage to settle with my father. Last night he and I talked—really talked for the first time in years, and when we were finished, my anger with him was gone. With my heart no longer filled with anger, I was able to see the love that was inside me…love for you.''

He placed his palms on either side of her face—a physical touch that had become so familiar to her. ''Joanna, I love you with all my heart. When you laugh, I feel your happiness inside of me. And when you cry, your tears scald my cheeks.''

Tears welled up inside her, tears of joy because she could see the transformation inside him, could feel his love radiating outward, bathing her in its beautiful glow.

''You said you wouldn't settle for less, that you wanted to marry a man who loved you, a man you loved. I'm asking you…I'm begging you to give me a chance, even if you don't love me. I swear I can love you enough for the both of us. I swear I'll do everything in my power to see that eventually you come to love me just a little.''

A tiny laugh escaped Joanna. She believed him. He loved her. He truly did love her.

''Joanna…I love you. Do you hear me? I love you!'' he exclaimed.

She wrapped her arms around his neck. "Eagle One, you are coming in loud and clear. You big lug," she exclaimed. "The main reason I didn't want to marry you was because *I love you!* I refused to marry you because I thought it was all just about the baby, and I couldn't be married to you, loving you like I do and knowing you would never love me."

He didn't give her an opportunity to say another word. He pulled her up against him as his mouth descended on hers. The kiss not only tasted of hunger and passion, but also of overwhelming love. If she hadn't believed his words of love, she could have believed the kiss.

"I'll tell you one thing," she said as his mouth left hers. "That, Lieutenant Commander Ramsey, was definitely a ten on my kiss scale."

He laughed and hugged her tighter. "Marry me, Joanna. Marry me and be my wife. Marry me and share your dreams with me. Together we'll create a home and raise children and put down the kind of roots you've always hungered for."

His words warmed every corner of her heart and she realized he was her future. He was her happiness.

"Yes, oh yes, Kyle," she agreed, and again he took possession of her mouth, his kiss filling her with hope and dreams and the assurance that their future together was going to be full of passion, and laughter, and love.

* * * * *

*Coming soon, don't miss Carla Cassidy's
next Intimate Moments novel!*

ONCE FORBIDDEN...

the next book in

THE DELANEY HEIRS

*miniseries from Carla Cassidy,
will be available in
November 2001.*

*And now, turn the page for
a sneak preview of*

BORN TO PROTECT

*by Virginia Kantra,
the third exciting installment of*

FIRSTBORN SONS,

*available from Intimate Moments
next month!*

Jack Dalton hitched his seabag on his shoulder. His uninjured shoulder, the one that wouldn't let him down. On the elevator door in front of him, some college banana with more sense of humor than respect for university property had slapped a bumper sticker.

Montana, The Last, Best Place...To Hide.

Jack's mouth quirked. Very funny. Funny and fitting. Not that he was hiding, whatever the old man accused him of. Drifting, maybe, but not hiding.

He prowled toward the stairs. The habits of physical conditioning were hard to break. And even the navy docs admitted there was nothing wrong with his legs. He could still climb to the lab before the elevator descended to the science-building lobby. He could still run six miles in thirty-nine minutes or less.

He could still stand for three hours in fifty-degree seawater without dropping or complaining.

What he couldn't do anymore was swim.

What he couldn't be anymore was a U.S. Navy SEAL.

Life was a bitch sometimes.

The stairwell—concrete and metal—caught every echo and threw it up and down. There was access onto each floor, through the basement and, he guessed, out onto the roof. He'd made only a cursory check of the building. He wasn't playing at point man. No one was relying on him anymore to spot bad guys and booby traps.

He hiked quickly and quietly up the stairs. Lots of stairs. His seabag rubbed the banister. A line from one of his younger sister's bedtime stories came back to him: "Once upon a time, a princess lived in a tower..."

Jack shook his head. Kid stuff. Unfortunately, the woman at the top of these steps was no fairy tale. Christina Sebastiani of Montebello might have fled the palace for life among the books and bunsen burners, but there was no getting around the fact that she was a real live princess. Montana University was an accredited ivory tower.

And the danger... If his father could be believed, that was real, too.

It was just Her Highness's tough luck that Jack was no knight in shining armor.

He exited the stairs and stalked the hall, counting doorways out of habit, noting angles from windows. Security sucked. Any thug with a gun and an agenda could have this floor pinned down in minutes. Not his problem, he reminded himself. He was only passing through.

A black plaque on the door identified the biology lab. A pane of frosted glass obscured his view of the room. Silently he turned the knob and slipped inside.

This was the place, all right. He did a quick scan of shelves packed with bottles and long black islands cluttered with glassware. Silhouetted against the painted cinder block, with two bunsen burners flaring and a couple dozen petri dishes laid out before her, stood a single slender figure in a white lab coat. Female. Blond. His hormones sat up and took notice. It had been a while, a long while, since he'd had a woman under him. Which was okay, but inconvenient.

She was a research scientist, his father had said during their brief, tense phone conversation. Jack had immediately pictured some dumpy, frumpy little woman in plastic goggles with her hair piled haphazardly on top of her head.

The goggles were there, pulled down around her neck. The hair was pulled back smoothly from her face and caught in a clip. And her face… He sucked in a breath. Her face had the cool, don't-touch-me perfection of a portrait under glass.

This was Princess Christina Sebastiani? Damn.

As he watched, she jiggled open the top of a glass bottle with the tip of her pinkie finger and held it to the flame. The intensity in her eyes—blue?—and the soft absorption of her mouth made his hands itch for his camera.

He wondered why he hadn't seen her photo splashed on the tabloids in the checkout line. She was as much a looker as the rest of the Sebastianis—the only royal to inherit the queen's blond beauty. But judging from the media coverage, her older sister, Julia, was the princess in the public eye, her younger sister, Anna, the one with the public's heart.

He waited while she poured stuff from the bottle into a petri dish, swirled it around and closed the container tight. No point in making her spill. She recapped the bottle, and he let his bag slide to the floor with a soft thump.

Christina jumped. Straightening her shoulders, she glared at him. Yeah, those eyes were blue, all right. Cool blue and hostile.

"You must be lost," she said. "The bus station is across from the stadium."

Jack admired her swift recovery. He even kind of liked her snotty tone. "I know. I just left there."

She looked him over. He knew what she saw: a big man in his early thirties, his convalescent pallor overlaid by a three-week tan and a day-old beard. His military haircut had mostly grown out. His jeans were creased with travel, his leather flight jacket powdered with dust. Not a reassuring sight for any woman working alone on an almost empty floor, let alone a princess.

"Then can I help you?" she asked.

He raised one eyebrow. "What did you have in mind?"

Her full lips pressed together. In annoyance? Or

fear? "You obviously don't belong here. If you don't leave, I'll have to call security."

"Maybe I am security," he suggested, just to see what she'd do.

"You're not in uniform. And I don't see a university ID tag."

She was cautious. That was in her favor. She was gorgeous. That was in his. For the first time, Jack began to think maybe he wasn't crazy for listening to his old man's suggestion that he drop in on the princess of Montebello....

*   *   *   *   *

**SILHOUETTE®
MAKES YOU
A STAR!**

Feel like a star with Silhouette.

We will fly you and a guest to New York City for an exciting weekend stay at a glamorous 5-star hotel. Experience a refreshing day at one of New York's trendiest spas and have your photo taken by a professional. Plus, receive $1,000 U.S. spending money!

Flowers...long walks...dinner for two... how does Silhouette Books make romance come alive for you?

Send us a script, with 500 words or less, along with visuals (only drawings, magazine cutouts or photographs or combination thereof). Show us how Silhouette Makes Your Love Come Alive. Be creative and have fun. No purchase necessary. All entries must be clearly marked with your name, address and telephone number. All entries will become property of Silhouette and are not returnable. **Contest closes September 28, 2001.**

Please send your entry to: **Silhouette Makes You a Star!**

In U.S.A.	In Canada
P.O. Box 9069	P.O. Box 637
Buffalo, NY, 14269-9069	Fort Erie, ON, L2A 5X3

Look for contest details on the next page, by visiting www.eHarlequin.com or request a copy by sending a self-addressed envelope to the applicable address above. Contest open to Canadian and U.S. residents who are 18 or over. Void where prohibited.

Silhouette®
Where love comes alive™

Our lucky winner's photo will appear in a Silhouette ad. Join the fun!

SRMYAS1

HARLEQUIN "SILHOUETTE MAKES YOU A STAR!" CONTEST 1308
OFFICIAL RULES
NO PURCHASE NECESSARY TO ENTER

1. To enter, follow directions published in the offer to which you are responding. Contest begins June 1, 2001, and ends on September 28, 2001. Entries must be postmarked by September 28, 2001, and received by October 5, 2001. Enter by hand-printing (or typing) on an 8 ½" x 11" piece of paper your name, address (including zip code), contest number/name and attaching a script containing <u>500 words or less, along with drawings, photographs or magazine cutouts, or combinations thereof</u> (i.e., collage) <u>on no larger than 9" x 12"</u> piece of paper, describing how the <u>Silhouette books make romance come alive for you.</u> Mail via first-class mail to: Harlequin "Silhouette Makes You a Star!" Contest 1308, (in the U.S.) P.O. Box 9069, Buffalo, NY 14269-9069, (in Canada) P.O. Box 637, Fort Erie, Ontario, Canada L2A 5X3. Limit one entry per person, household or organization.

2. Contests will be judged by a panel of members of the Harlequin editorial, marketing and public relations staff. Fifty percent of criteria will be judged against script and fifty percent will be judged against drawing, photographs and/or magazine cutouts. Judging criteria will be based on the following:

   - Sincerity—25%
   - Originality and Creativity—50%
   - Emotionally Compelling—25%

   In the event of a tie, duplicate prizes will be awarded. Decisions of the judges are final.

3. All entries become the property of Torstar Corp. and may be used for future promotional purposes. Entries will not be returned. No responsibility is assumed for lost, late, illegible, incomplete, inaccurate, nondelivered or misdirected mail.

4. Contest open only to residents of the U.S. <u>(except Puerto Rico)</u> and Canada who are 18 years of age or older, and is void wherever prohibited by law; all applicable laws and regulations apply. Any litigation within the Province of Quebec respecting the conduct or organization of a publicity contest may be submitted to the Régie des alcools, des courses et des jeux for a ruling. Any litigation respecting the awarding of a prize may be submitted to the Régie des alcools, des courses et des jeux only for the purpose of helping the parties reach a settlement. Employees and immediate family members of Torstar Corp. and D. L. Blair, Inc., their affiliates, subsidiaries and all other agencies, entities and persons connected with the use, marketing or conduct of this contest are not eligible to enter. Taxes on prizes are the sole responsibility of the winner. Acceptance of any prize offered constitutes permission to use winner's name, photograph or other likeness for the purposes of advertising, trade and promotion on behalf of Torstar Corp., its affiliates and subsidiaries without further compensation to the winner, unless prohibited by law.

5. Winner will be determined no later than November 30, 2001, and will be notified by mail. Winner will be required to sign and return an Affidavit of Eligibility/Release of Liability/Publicity Release form within 15 days after winner notification. Noncompliance within that time period may result in disqualification and an alternative winner may be selected. All travelers must execute a Release of Liability prior to ticketing and must possess required travel documents (e.g., passport, photo ID) where applicable. Trip must be booked by December 31, 2001, and completed within one year of notification. No substitution of prize permitted by winner. Torstar Corp. and D. L. Blair, Inc., their parents, affiliates and subsidiaries are not responsible for errors in printing of contest, entries and/or game pieces. In the event of printing or other errors that may result in unintended prize values or duplication of prizes, all affected game pieces or entries shall be null and void. **Purchase or acceptance of a product offer does not improve your chances of winning.**

6. Prizes: (1) Grand Prize—A 2-night/3-day trip for two (2) to New York City, including round-trip coach air transportation nearest winner's home and hotel accommodations (double occupancy) at The Plaza Hotel, a glamorous afternoon makeover at <u>a trendy New York spa</u>, $1,000 in U.S. spending money and an opportunity to <u>have a professional photo taken and appear in a Silhouette advertisement</u> (approximate retail value: $7,000). (10) Ten Runner-Up Prizes of gift packages (retail value $50 ea.). Prizes consist of only those items listed as part of the prize. Limit one prize per person. Prize is valued in U.S. currency.

7. For the name of the winner (available after December 31, 2001) send a self-addressed, stamped envelope to: Harlequin "Silhouette Makes You a Star!" Contest 1197 Winners, P.O. Box 4200 Blair, NE 68009-4200 or you may access the www.eHarlequin.com Web site through February 28, 2002.

Contest sponsored by Torstar Corp., P.O Box 9042, Buffalo, NY 14269-9042.

SRMYAS2

Revitalize!

With help from
Silhouette's *New York Times*
bestselling authors
and receive a

FREE

Refresher Kit!

LUCIA IN LOVE by Heather Graham
and LION ON THE PROWL by Kasey Michaels

LOVE SONG FOR A RAVEN by Elizabeth Lowell
and THE FIVE-MINUTE BRIDE by Leanne Banks

MACKENZIE'S PLEASURE by Linda Howard
and DEFENDING HIS OWN by Beverly Barton

DARING MOVES by Linda Lael Miller
and MARRIAGE ON DEMAND by Susan Mallery

Don't miss out!

*Look for this exciting promotion, on sale in
October 2001 at your favorite retail outlet.
See inside books for details.*

Only from

Where love comes alive™

Visit Silhouette at www.eHarlequin.com   PSNCP-POP